Sylvie D

LA JE
FILLE VENUE
DU FROID

Illustrations
de Daniel Sylvestre

la courte échelle
Les éditions de la courte échelle inc.

Les éditions de la courte échelle inc.
5243, boul. Saint-Laurent
Montréal (Québec) H2T 1S4

Conception graphique:
Derome design inc.

Révision des textes:
Pierre Phaneuf

Dépôt légal, 1er trimestre 1997
Bibliothèque nationale du Québec

La courte échelle est inscrite au programme de subvention globale du
Conseil des Arts du Canada et bénéficie de l'appui de la SODEC.

Données de catalogage avant publication (Canada)

Desrosiers, Sylvie

    La jeune fille venue du froid

    (Roman Jeunesse; RJ64)

    ISBN 2-89021-283-1

    I. Sylvestre, Daniel. II. Titre. III. Collection.

PS8557.E8745J48   1997   jC843'.54   C96-941221-5
PS9557.E8745J48   1997
PZ23.D47Je   1997

Sylvie Desrosiers

À part rire et faire rire, Sylvie Desrosiers passe beaucoup de temps à écrire. Elle a fait ses débuts au magazine *Croc* et elle rédige, à l'occasion, des textes pour la télévision.

C'est elle qui a créé le célèbre chien Notdog et les inséparables jeunes détectives, dont chaque nouvelle aventure est attendue avec impatience. Certains de ses livres ont été traduits en chinois, en grec, en italien et en arabe. En plus de la littérature jeunesse, elle a publié deux romans pour adultes et trois recueils humoristiques. Et bien sûr, elle se garde beaucoup de temps pour jouer avec son fils et son chien Mozart.

La jeune fille venue du froid est le treizième roman qu'elle publie à la courte échelle.

Daniel Sylvestre

C'est bien jeune que Daniel Sylvestre s'est mis à dessiner. Et ce goût ne l'a jamais quitté, puisqu'il est devenu illustrateur. Il a travaillé à des films d'animation et il a fait de l'illustration éditoriale pour des revues comme *Châtelaine*, *L'actualité* et *Croc*, ainsi que du travail graphique et des affiches publicitaires. Bref, il s'amuse en travaillant et il amuse, par le fait même, petits et grands. Dans ses temps libres, il joue de la guitare.

Daniel Sylvestre a reçu le prix Québec-Wallonie-Bruxelles pour *Je suis Zunik* et il a été plusieurs fois finaliste du prix du Conseil des Arts.

La jeune fille venue du froid est le dixième roman qu'il illustre à la courte échelle, en plus des neuf albums de la série Zunik et des couvertures de plusieurs romans de la collection Roman+.

De la même auteure, à la courte échelle

Collection Roman Jeunesse

Série Notdog:
La patte dans le sac
Qui a peur des fantômes?
Le mystère du lac Carré
Où sont passés les dinosaures?
Méfiez-vous des monstres marins
Mais qui va trouver le trésor?
Faut-il croire à la magie?
Les princes ne sont pas tous charmants
Qui veut entrer dans la légende?

Collection Roman+

Quatre jours de liberté
Les cahiers d'Élisabeth
Le long silence

Chapitre I
Le commencement de la faim

Jamais on n'avait connu un hiver aussi froid. Par cette belle nuit étoilée, personne au village de X ne met le nez dehors.

Depuis le matin, les Cantons de l'Est sont envahis par un froid sibérien: le thermomètre est descendu à moins quarante degrés. Ce qui, pour le plus grand bonheur des enfants, a provoqué la fermeture des écoles, aucun autobus scolaire n'ayant pu démarrer.

Les rares courageux qui ont tenté une sortie ont vite rebroussé chemin, car un vent glacial réussissait à pénétrer les duvets les plus épais.

Même les chiens habitués à dormir dehors ont été pris en pitié par leurs maîtres et ronflent dans la chaleur des cuisines.

Engourdi par la froidure, le village a des allures de carte postale. Seule la fumée des cheminées rappelle qu'il y a de la vie, ici.

Donc, par cette belle nuit étoilée, personne dans le village n'apercevra la jeune fille.

Bien emmitouflée dans une fourrure soyeuse, elle avance à pas lents dans les rues tranquilles, attentive au moindre bruit. Elle regarde partout à la fois, cherchant l'ombre, évitant l'éclairage des réverbères.

Elle marche, mais la neige ne crisse pas sous son pas. Elle respire, mais aucun son n'émane d'elle. À peine pourrait-on remarquer une buée épaisse sortir de sa bouche si, évidemment, il y avait quelqu'un pour la voir.

Elle passe devant la caisse populaire, le restaurant Steve La Patate, le garage Joe Auto. Elle dépasse l'auberge Sous mon toit, d'où lui parviennent les rires des clients bien au chaud devant un bon feu. Puis, elle arrive à destination. Elle s'arrête devant la boucherie Au Carnivore.

Bien sûr, la porte est verrouillée. Alors la jeune fille contourne le commerce et essaye d'entrer par la porte de derrière. À

cause du gel, le boucher, M. Leboeuf, n'a jamais pu la fermer à clef. Mais il s'est dit que personne au village ne viendrait le voler. Par un froid pareil, même les voleurs restent au chaud en dedans.

La jeune fille entre dans la boucherie, s'approche du comptoir. Deux minutes plus tard, elle ressort avec un gros paquet caché sous son manteau.

Chapitre II
On traîne
en traîneau

Le lendemain matin, le réchauffement tant attendu ne vint pas. Mais pas question d'annuler ce qui était prévu pour ce samedi de janvier. Les inséparables feront donc cette randonnée en traîneau que Jocelyne a gagnée.

C'était au cours d'un tournoi de jeu de poches, qui avait lieu au Club de l'âge d'or. Elle y était allée pour faire plaisir à son oncle, organisateur de la compétition. Elle avait remporté le grand prix, à la suite d'un tirage au sort. Elle était rentrée chez elle, ravie.

Ce matin, elle l'est un peu moins.

— Pour une fois que je gagne quelque chose, grommelle-t-elle, en enfilant sa troisième paire de bas thermos.

À côté d'elle, Notdog, son chien, bien connu comme le chien le plus laid du village, sautille, tout excité. Il sait que quelque chose se prépare et il a bien l'intention d'y participer. Il bondit sur le fauteuil près de la fenêtre, regarde dehors, jappe. Une énorme boule grise surmontée d'une tuque à pompon rouge arrive. Avant même d'entendre sonner à la porte, Jocelyne ouvre:

— Wow! Tu as mis le manteau de ton père?

— Celui de mon grand-père, répond Agnès à travers le foulard mouillé et glacé à l'endroit où il couvre la bouche et le nez.

Jocelyne a à peine le temps de faire entrer son amie que déjà une forme élancée s'approche. Elle est couverte d'une fourrure brune, de bottes de motoneige, d'une tuque péruvienne, et elle avance d'un pas incertain, puisqu'elle ne peut rien voir avec ses lunettes embuées. La forme entre. Les filles éclatent de rire.

— Riez tant que vous voulez. Mais c'est pas de ma faute. Ma mère m'a obligé à mettre son manteau de rat casqué, se lamente John, humilié.

— Musqué, John, le mot c'est musqué,

le corrige Agnès, comme elle le fait chaque fois que le garçon commet une faute
de français.

— Tu parles d'une journée pour sortir
en traîneau, se plaint Jocelyne en remon-
tant la fermeture éclair de son habit de ski.

— Au moins, il n'y aura personne pour
me voir arrangé comme ça, dit John, phi-
losophe.

Agnès resserre son foulard:

— Tout le monde est prêt? On y va!

Et Jocelyne, la jolie brune, Agnès, la rousse qui porte des broches*, et John, l'Anglais blond à lunettes, sortent courageusement dans le froid. Notdog s'élance à leur suite mais s'arrête net: «Oh oh! Ça me semble un peu frisquet. Est-ce que j'ai vraiment si envie que ça de les suivre?»

Il va faire demi-tour, mais Jocelyne le siffle. Et il n'y a pas un seul temps de cochon sur terre qui le fera passer outre à l'appel de sa maîtresse adorée.

* * *

À leur arrivée aux écuries Palomino, leur guide, M. Palomino lui-même, est en train d'atteler les chevaux. Fort habilement, il fait reculer les deux immenses bêtes vers le traîneau. Il y a Jim, le gris, et Jack, le noir, de nobles percherons à peine âgés de huit ans, mais pesant pas moins de neuf cents kilos. Chacun.

N'ayant pas l'air le moins du monde incommodé par le froid, M. Palomino ac-

*Appareil orthodontique.

cueille les enfants joyeusement:

— Parlez-moi de ça! Des braves qui n'ont pas peur de se geler le nombril! Allez, hop! montez! Faut faire bouger les chevaux pour qu'ils se réchauffent!

Les inséparables se collent les uns aux autres sur la banquette couverte d'une épaisse peau de mouton. Une autre peau, de chat sauvage celle-là, sert à les abrier.

Un peu inquiet, Notdog appuie ses pattes sur le bord de la carriole. Comme les enfants, c'est la première fois qu'il fait une randonnée en traîneau tiré par des chevaux. «Pas sûr, pas sûr que j'ai bien fait de venir», pense-t-il, constatant que cette drôle de voiture n'a pas de roues.

Il ne fait pas non plus confiance aux chevaux. «Plus c'est gros, plus c'est nono, ces affaires-là», se dit-il. Mais voilà que le conducteur crie:

— Hue!

Et la voiture se met à glisser doucement.

Bientôt, Jim et Jack trottent en cadence dans ce qui est, l'été, un champ de blé. Une buée épaisse sort de leurs naseaux.

On entend le schich! schich! du traîneau sur la neige, le tintement des grelots et les ordres de M. Palomino.

Puis, ils s'enfoncent dans une pinède, avançant lentement sur un chemin normalement emprunté par des tracteurs. Des traces de lapins et de chevreuils le traversent en divers endroits, signes que la forêt, malgré le froid, grouille de vie.

Peu intéressé par la nature, Notdog se faufile sous une peau aux longs poils étalée aux pieds des enfants.

Jocelyne le remarque:

— Tu as froid, mon gros? C'est vrai que tu es pas mal douillet.

Mais Notdog n'a que faire des insultes. L'important, c'est la chaleur.

— Tu n'auras pas froid sous cette peau-là. C'est une peau de quoi, en fait? demande Agnès.

— Une peau de loup, répond M. Palomino.

— De loup? C'est vous qui l'avez tué? s'inquiète John.

M. Palomino tire sur les rênes pour stopper les chevaux et les faire reposer un instant:

— Non, je ne l'ai pas tué. Il n'y a pas de loups par ici.

— Vous êtes sûr de ça? veut savoir Jocelyne. Moi, j'aimerais bien voir un loup.

Leur guide rit:

— Mais, chère, la seule place où tu peux voir un loup sans courir de risques, c'est dans un zoo. J'espère que tu n'en rencontreras jamais un face à face. De toute façon, il n'y a pas de danger que ça t'arrive parce qu'il n'y a plus de loups au sud du Saint-Laurent depuis fort longtemps. Cette peau-là vient d'un de mes cousins du lac Saint-Jean. Allez, il faut repartir, sinon les chevaux vont être malades. Jim! Jack! Hue!

Le traîneau s'enfonce un peu plus dans les bois d'une réelle splendeur. Les branches des sapins sont lourdes de neige, et le soleil fait des cristaux un feu d'artifice.

Les enfants apprécient le spectacle, posent toutes sortes de questions à M. Palomino. Puis, ils regardent en silence défiler le paysage. Soudain, Notdog s'échappe de sa cachette.

— Tiens, tu n'as plus froid maintenant, dit Jocelyne.

Mais ce qui a fait sortir son chien, ce n'est pas la température, c'est une drôle d'odeur. Une odeur qu'il n'arrive pas à identifier, puisqu'elle lui est inconnue. D'instinct, il grogne.

— Qu'est-ce qu'il y a? s'alarme Agnès.

Les enfants regardent de tous bords, tous côtés, ne voient rien. Notdog grogne encore. M. Palomino, qui garde son calme, les rassure:

— Il a dû sentir un coyote. Ça, il y en a par ici. Pas de danger. De toute façon, on retourne. Ça vous a plu?

Les inséparables se disent ravis de la randonnée.

Alors que les chevaux prennent le chemin de l'écurie, tout près dans les bois, des yeux perçants suivent le traîneau.

Ce ne sont pas des yeux de coyote.

Chapitre III

Qui vole un oeuf, vole-t-il un rôti de boeuf?

Le dimanche matin c'est encore pire que le samedi. Le vent venu du pôle Nord semble résolu à rester au village quelque temps avant d'aller souffler un peu plus à l'est. Les rues sont désertes, sauf aux alentours de la tabagie tenue par l'oncle de Jocelyne, Édouard Duchesne.

Le dimanche matin c'est sacré pour plusieurs personnes, et rien ne les empêcherait d'acheter leur journal. Justement, M. Palomino entre.

À l'intérieur, Jocelyne aide à servir les clients. Elle est chargée des opérations à la caisse. De son côté, Notdog fait cent fois le tour des allées, à la recherche de nouvelles odeurs.

— Brrr! une chance que votre tour de traîneau n'était pas ce matin! Je pense que je l'aurais annulé! lance M. Palomino en frissonnant.

— De toute façon, j'aurais gagé un dix que tes chevaux auraient refusé de sortir, rétorque Édouard Duchesne en riant.

— Ouais. Surtout après la nuit qu'ils ont passée, répond M. Palomino en prenant son journal.

Jocelyne enregistre 0,75$ sur la caisse:

— Ils ont été malades?

— Non. Ils sont devenus fous! Ils piaffaient et ils hennissaient comme si le feu était pris. Je suis allé voir. Ils étaient complètement paniqués. Mais j'ai eu beau chercher, je n'ai rien vu qui aurait pu les effrayer.

— Ils ont peut-être entendu quelque chose, un bruit inconnu, un animal, suggère l'oncle Édouard.

— J'ai fait le tour de l'écurie. Rien. Ils ont fini par se calmer, et je suis retourné me coucher. Pour moi, ils ont vu des Martiens.

Attiré par les nouvelles odeurs enveloppant le propriétaire de chevaux, Notdog vient le renifler. M. Palomino se penche pour caresser le chien le plus laid du village. En même temps, la porte s'ouvre, et le vent s'engouffre dans la boutique. Jocelyne remonte le col de son chandail de grosse laine: «Mais qu'est-ce qu'il fait ici, lui?»

Les oreilles de sa tuque de laine ballottantes, le cou à l'air, le jeans déchiré aux genoux, les bottes de caoutchouc détachées et le blouson de laine trop court, Bob «Les Oreilles» Bigras fait son entrée. Le motard local exhibe son plus beau sourire, qui révèle ses dents cariées:

— Heille! On se croirait dans le Sud, aujourd'hui!

Constatant l'air sidéré des autres, il ajoute:

— Dans le pôle Sud!

Et il éclate d'un gros rire gras.

— Ils t'ont laissé sortir de prison, toi? demande Édouard Duchesne.

— Minute, là! Ça fait longtemps que je suis sorti. On reste pas longtemps quand c'est juste pour un petit... emprunt... de moto. Mais avec le temps qu'il fait, j'aurais aimé mieux qu'ils me gardent.

Bob choisit deux petits gâteaux, des bonbons et de la gomme, rien pour améliorer sa dentition.

La porte s'ouvre de nouveau. Cette fois-ci, c'est le boucher qui apparaît. Au même moment, le téléphone sonne. Édouard répond:

— Ah! bonjour chef! Oui... Quoi! Pauvre lui!... Combien?... Non! Pas lui aussi!... Même chez Fernande?... Oui, bien sûr, si j'entends quoi que ce soit, je vous le dirai... Oui. Vous ne pensez tout de même pas que... Oui, s'il y a des traces... D'accord. Promis.

— Qu'est-ce qui se passe, mon oncle?

— Les Légaré se sont fait voler dix poules. Les Brunelle ont perdu deux oies. Et trois des moutons de Fernande ont disparu.

— Des indices sur les coupables? demande M. Palomino.

— Des traces, seulement. Des traces de loup.

Jocelyne intervient:

— Mais il n'y a pas de loups par ici, hein monsieur Palomino?

C'est Édouard Duchesne qui répond:

— Non. En principe. Mais il y a des traces, ça, c'est certain. Ce qui veut dire: défense de s'éloigner.

Jocelyne proteste:

— Je n'ai pas peur.

Bob Les Oreilles se met à ricaner:

— Attends d'en rencontrer un et qu'il te saute à la gorge et qu'il commence à te dépecer vivante...

— Ça suffit, Bob! Arrête de faire peur à ma nièce.

Bob marmonne:

— Moi, je voulais juste vous aider à la convaincre... Euh... Combien ça vaut, une peau de loup?

M. Palomino lui lance un regard froid:

— N'y pense même pas, Les Oreilles. Et même s'il y avait un loup, dis-toi que la chasse en est interdite.

— Oh! Moi, je demandais ça, juste comme ça...

Et Bob enfourne un gâteau.

M. Leboeuf, resté silencieux depuis son entrée, toussote:

— Eh bien moi, je me suis fait voler neuf kilos de viande.

— Oh non! pas des traces de loup dans le village en plus! s'inquiète Édouard.

— Non, des traces de pas bien humains.

— Tu as une caméra de surveillance, non? demande M. Palomino.

— Oui.

— Alors tu vas voir ton voleur sur vidéo.

M. Leboeuf soupire:

— C'est que... c'est arrivé la nuit. Il faisait noir, l'image est tellement floue qu'on ne peut même pas voir si c'est un homme ou une femme.

M. Leboeuf rougit un peu. Mais personne ne s'en aperçut.

Chapitre IV

L'expert expose
son... inexpérience

La seule personne qui réussit à suer aujourd'hui est Steve, de chez Steve La Patate. Le casse-croûte du village est en effet bondé pour le repas de midi.

Justement, il est en train de rédiger une commande:

— Alors, une poutine double sauce barbecue, un hot-dog ketchup-chou et une pointe de pizza hawaïenne. Pour boire, avec ça?

— Trois jus de raisin, répond Jocelyne.

— Un petit pain trempé dans la sauce brune pour Notdog?

— Oui, oui, comme d'habitude.

Jocelyne rejoint Agnès et John assis à une table près de la fenêtre. Mais il y a tellement de buée dans le restaurant qu'il est impossible de voir à l'extérieur.

Bien sûr, la jeune maîtresse de Notdog a raconté à ses amis tout ce qu'elle a appris à la tabagie le matin même. D'ailleurs, la nouvelle de la présence possible d'un loup a fait le tour du village, et l'interdiction de s'éloigner s'applique à tous les enfants.

— Ça va être plate de ne pas pouvoir aller en forêt, se plaint John.

— Depuis quand veux-tu aller dans le bois? Tu refuses toujours de sortir quand il fait froid! lui fait remarquer Agnès.

— C'est bizarre: c'est quand c'est in-verti que j'en ai le plus envie.

— Interdit, John, pas inverti, le reprend Agnès.

À ce moment-là, la porte s'ouvre pour laisser entrer d'abord un inconnu qui va immédiatement au comptoir et, ensuite, un petit bout de garçon, tenant la main de sa mère.

— Regardez, c'est le petit Dédé La-pointe, dit Jocelyne. Mais qu'est-ce qu'il a? On dirait qu'il pleure.

Deux longues traces de glace traversent les joues de Dédé. Patiemment et douce-ment, Mme Lapointe installe son fils à une

30

table près des inséparables. Elle lui enlève son manteau, lui demande ce qu'il veut manger et va passer sa commande à Steve.

L'inconnu s'assoit lui aussi tout près des enfants, à la dernière table libre. Lentement, il mange sa soupe bouillante. Steve fait signe aux inséparables, et John va chercher leur repas.

Dédé renifle et essuie son nez avec la manche de son coton ouaté du zoo de Granby. Jocelyne vient s'asseoir à côté de lui:

— Qu'est-ce qui se passe, Dédé? Pourquoi es-tu si malheureux?

— On m'a volé mon lapin, pleurniche le bambin.

— Oh! pas Dents Coupantes! Comment ça se fait?

— Sais pas. Je l'ai mis dehors cinq minutes pour qu'il prenne l'air. Quand j'ai voulu le rentrer, sa cage était ouverte. Et lui parti.

— Peut-être que tu avais mal refermé la cage?

— Jamais! Je fais très attention à Dents Coupantes! répond le garçon, insulté.

Il essuie une larme, réfléchit. Puis, le plus sérieusement du monde, il ajoute:

— Je pense que c'est ou bien le loup qui l'a mangé, ou bien un magnat de la fourrure qui l'a enlevé.

Les inséparables font un effort pour ne pas rire. Ils connaissent bien la tendance du garçon à fabuler. Ce n'est pas la même chose pour l'inconnu, qui ne peut s'empêcher de sourire.

— Ce n'est certainement pas le loup, mon garçon, dit-il la cuillère en l'air.

Les enfants se tournent vers lui.

— Vous êtes bien sûr? demande Dédé, méfiant.

— Absolument certain. Les loups ne s'aventurent pas jusqu'aux maisons d'un village. Je me présente: Jean É. Chassé, grand spécialiste des loups du bureau régional du ministère de la Faune. Tout le monde me surnomme Ti-Loup.

— Wow! Vous en avez déjà attrapé? s'exclame John, impressionné.

— Euh, non, euh, je dois dire que, évidemment, comme il n'y a pas de loups au sud du Saint-Laurent...

— Qu'est-ce que ça fait, alors, un expert en loup dans un endroit où il n'y en a pas? demande Agnès.

— Eh bien, j'observe les chevreuils, je

suis leurs pistes grâce à leurs crottes.

Les enfants se regardent et savent que chacun pense la même chose: voilà un métier pas trop ragoûtant.

— Vous venez pour le loup? s'enquiert Jocelyne.

— Oui. Le supposé loup. On m'a demandé de venir sur les lieux tôt ce matin. J'aurais peut-être enfin la chance d'en attraper un. Euh, pour le relocaliser, bien sûr.

La mère de Dédé arrive avec leur dîner. Jean É. Chassé replonge dans sa soupe. Les inséparables ainsi que Notdog font honneur à leur repas mais, bientôt, ce dernier gratte la porte.

— Oh! Pipi, constate sa maîtresse, qui s'habille pour sortir avec lui.

Comme d'habitude, Notdog s'élance à la recherche de l'endroit idéal. Il aboutit derrière la boucherie, où se trouve une belle poubelle bien pleine. Jocelyne n'a pas le temps de le rejoindre qu'il est déjà dedans, y léchant quelque chose.

— Notdog, ôte-toi de là!

Mais c'est trop bon. Jocelyne vient tirer son chien par le collier. Machinalement, elle regarde dans la poubelle ce dont se

régalait son chien: un steak à moitié
mangé.

— C'est dégueulasse! Tiens...

À côté du steak, une cassette vidéo.

— Elle a l'air neuve. Je me demande ce
qu'il y a d'enregistré dessus.

Elle regarde à gauche, à droite, pour être

bien certaine que personne ne la voie fouiller dans une poubelle. Elle sort la cassette, la nettoie avec de la neige.

— Ça nous fera quelque chose à faire cet après-midi. Viens, Notdog.

Elle rejoint ses amis à la sortie du restaurant. Dix minutes plus tard, dans le sous-sol chez Agnès, ils visionnent le vidéo.

— Hé! c'est la boucherie Au Carnivore! Regardez, on voit les clients! s'exclame Agnès.

Défile devant eux une partie du village: Jean Caisse, le gérant de la caisse populaire, s'achète du foie. Mimi Demi, la gérante du Mimi Bar and Grill, commande du steak haché, le chef de police, un gigot d'agneau. Et ainsi de suite. Puis, M. Lebocuf éteint les lumières.

— Il ferme. Il n'y aura plus rien, dit Jocelyne.

— On ne sait jamais. Peut-être qu'il y a des monstres ou des vampires qui viennent la nuit, dit Agnès en pouffant de rire.

La cassette continue de se dérouler un bout de temps, sans que rien n'arrive. C'est John qui la voit le premier:

— Hé! là! regardez!

Sur l'écran, on voit très bien une personne en manteau de fourrure. En y regardant de plus près, les enfants aperçoivent une jeune fille.

— Ça alors! Vous avez vu la quantité de viande qu'elle prend? Il y en a pour nourrir quarante personnes! observe Agnès.

Jocelyne réfléchit tout haut:

— M. Leboeuf a dit qu'on ne voyait rien sur la cassette. Pourquoi a-t-il menti?

— Et jeté la cassette... ajoute John, perplexe.

**

Ce soir-là, John ne réussit pas à dormir. Cette histoire de loup l'excite beaucoup. Il s'imagine rencontrant un loup, le caressant, communiquant avec lui, même.

Mais il a peur aussi. Peur que quelqu'un veuille tuer l'animal. Jocelyne n'a-t-elle pas dit que Bob Les Oreilles Bigras avait demandé combien valait une peau de loup? Avec Bob, il faut toujours se méfier.

Et il y a cette jeune fille mystérieuse.

À l'écran, on pouvait distinguer son visage malgré la pénombre. Elle était si jolie... Et ses yeux! Deux petites flammes où brillait ce qui devait être la peur d'être découverte.

Qui était-elle? À qui destinait-elle toute cette viande? John sent battre son coeur. Ce qui lui paraît bien étrange, à douze ans.

Il se lève, n'allume pas la lumière de sa chambre. Il va à la fenêtre pour regarder la lune dans ce ciel clair d'hiver. Avec l'arrivée de la nuit, la neige a pris une teinte bleutée. La rue est déserte... Sauf pour cette ombre qui avance prudemment.

— C'est elle! s'exclame John.

Il dévale l'escalier en quatrième vitesse, enfile bottes et manteau par-dessus son pyjama, et se précipite dehors.

La jeune fille marche au bout de la rue. John court, puis ralentit; il ne veut pas l'effrayer. La neige crisse sous ses pas. Il a l'impression que sa respiration fait un bruit épouvantable. Celle qu'il suit s'arrête soudain: elle l'a entendu. Elle se retourne.

— Mademoiselle, je... Il ne faut pas avoir peur de moi. Je veux juste vous parler, commence John.

Il fait quelques pas. Elle ne bouge pas.

— Je ne vous veux pas de mal. Seulement savoir qui vous êtes.

Il se rapproche doucement.

— Je... je vous promets que je ne vais pas vous annoncer.

Il veut dire dénoncer. Mais la jeune fille ne le reprend pas. Elle se met à courir, prend à droite à l'angle de la rue. John s'élance, mais arrivé à l'intersection il ne voit plus personne. Il a beau chercher partout, elle a disparu.

Troublé et déçu, il rebrousse chemin. Un frisson l'envahit: il s'aperçoit qu'il n'a pas attaché son manteau. Il presse le pas, regarde ses pieds en marchant.

Il s'arrête net. Car dans la rue il distingue des traces. «Sûrement des traces de chien», espère-t-il. Il accélère le pas. Il a maintenant la très nette impression d'entendre le souffle d'un animal. Il ne se retourne pas, prend ses jambes à son cou et claque derrière lui la porte de sa maison.

En se glissant dans son lit, il se rend compte qu'il tremble comme une feuille.

Chapitre V

Où on cherche un loup, une jeune fille, un prétexte et son chemin

Marchant de long en large devant son pupitre, Mlle Descartes, la prof de géographie, pose des questions à ses élèves:

— Quelle est la capitale de la France? Jocelyne?

— Paris.

— Bien. Quel pays a comme capitale Reykjavik? Agnès?

— L'Islande.

— Bien. Comment appelle-t-on le détroit qui sépare l'Amérique du Nord de l'Asie? John?... John? Le détroit de...?

— Pardon? Je n'ai pas compris la question.

— Tu étais dans la lune encore!

C'est à peine si John entend Mlle Descartes dire «Béring». Il est fatigué et, oui, dans la lune. Ou plutôt dans les images de la nuit précédente.

C'est alors que deux notes de musique se font entendre dans le haut-parleur de la classe. Ce qui signifie qu'on va leur communiquer un message.

Le directeur de l'école lui-même s'adresse aux élèves. C'est avec regret qu'il leur apprend que le système de chauffage de l'école s'avère défectueux. Il n'a d'autre choix que de les renvoyer chez eux jusqu'à ce que les réparations nécessaires soient effectuées.

L'école est alors secouée de cris de joie venus de tous les étages. Il ne faut pas plus de dix minutes pour qu'une horde d'enfants excités dévale les escaliers et se rue dehors. En espérant, bien sûr, que le problème de chauffage ne sera pas réglé avant le mois de juin. Au plus tôt.

— Qu'est-ce qu'on va faire? demande Jocelyne à ses amis, en sautillant partout.

— On pourrait chercher la mystérieuse

jeune fille. Je suis certaine que ça ferait plaisir à John... ironise Agnès, qui sent naître chez son ami un drôle de sentiment.

John rougit. Agnès enchaîne:

— On pourrait aussi partir à la recherche du loup.

— Mais on n'a pas le droit! lance John.

***

Dans la ville voisine, Bob Les Oreilles Bigras fouine chez un armurier. Comme le vendeur lui trouve une tête de délinquant, il se méfie de Bob.

— Qu'est-ce qu'on peut faire pour vous, monsieur?

— Oh! Je regarde. Euh... c'est combien, un fusil de chasse?

— Ça dépend du modèle.

Et le vendeur se lance dans la description des caractéristiques de toutes les armes qu'il a en magasin.

— C'est pour quelle sorte de gibier?

— Du gros, répond évasivement Bob.

— Du chevreuil? De l'orignal?

«Y'est donc fatigant avec ses questions, lui!» pense Bob, qui cherche désespérément un prétexte pour justifier son désir de se procurer un fusil.

— C'est pour mes vaches, finit-il par dire. Il y en a un paquet de malades. La maladie de la vache folle. Je dois les abattre.

Regardant Bob Les Oreilles de haut en bas, le vendeur se dit que ce gars-là n'a probablement pas plus de vaches que lui un dinosaure.

— Monsieur a un permis, évidemment.

— Un permis? Euh, évidemment.

Bob fouille dans ses poches:

— C'est niaiseux, mais je l'ai oublié chez nous. Ça fait que, je pense que je vais revenir.

Bob tourne les talons, sort de la boutique. Il enfonce ses mains dans ses poches, crache un bon coup et s'en va en se demandant comment régler son problème.

***

Au presbytère du village, M. Leboeuf, le boucher, cherche des renseignements. Le curé Martel promène son index le long des registres de baptême:

— J'ai bien une Agathe Duruisseau. Baptisée en 1955.

— C'est elle, oui.

— Une fille, vous dites. Autour de quatorze, quinze ans. Bien sûr, elle doit avoir été baptisée pour figurer dans les registres. Sinon, il faudra vous renseigner à la Direction de l'état civil.

— Mais ça prendra des mois! s'exclame le boucher.

— C'est comme ça, les services gouvernementaux.

Le curé passe en revue tous les baptêmes effectués entre 1979 et 1985.

— Ah! Duruisseau, Jacinthe. Née le 12 juin 1980.

M. Leboeuf retient son souffle.

— Mère: ah, c'est une Carmen Shaw. Ce n'est pas ça... Je regrette, je n'ai rien.

— Merci, dit le boucher, déçu.

Il ouvre la porte du presbytère et, en la refermant, il entend le curé Martel lui souhaiter bonne chance à l'état civil.

***

Dans sa chambre de l'auberge Sous mon toit, Jean É. Chassé prépare son attirail.

«Mes raquettes, mes bottes, mes lunettes de soleil, mes bas de laine, mon manteau de duvet, mes gants sans bouts de doigts, mes mitaines. Bon.

«Le traîneau est dehors, tout fin prêt. Mon fusil, le viseur, les seringues, les sédatifs, les allumettes. Bon.

«Ah oui! La boussole. Mais où est-ce que j'ai pu la mettre? Je ne peux pas me promener en forêt sans ma boussole!»

Ti-Loup cherche partout. Dans sa valise, dans ses bas, dans ses poches, sous le matelas du lit, même. Il ne la trouve pas.

— Tant pis! dit-il tout haut. Je finirai bien par trouver mon chemin. On ne m'appelle pas Ti-Loup pour rien.

***

À l'orée de la forêt, les inséparables hésitent. Si jamais leurs parents apprennent qu'ils sont allés dans les bois, ils n'auront plus le droit de sortir. Point à la ligne.

Mais voilà, les deux filles n'ont absolument pas peur du loup, affirment-elles. Sans parler de Notdog, toujours prêt pour l'aventure. Quant à John, il s'est un peu fait tirer l'oreille: il n'a pas oublié sa frayeur de la nuit. Mais quand il fait jour, tout paraît tellement moins dangereux!

Chaussés de raquettes, ils marchent lentement.

— Et s'il y avait plusieurs loups? se demande Jocelyne, tout de même un peu inquiète.

John répond en essayant de se rassurer lui-même:

— On les aurait entendus: ça hurle, une émeute.

— Une meute, John, pas une émeute, le reprend Agnès. De toute façon, euh, on n'ira pas si loin que ça.

Elle aussi est finalement un peu craintive.

À mesure qu'ils avancent, ils se sentent pourtant plus confiants. Il fait si beau soleil! Il n'y a presque pas de vent, et des geais bleus tournoient dans les cèdres enneigés. Il y a bien çà et là quelques traces de lièvres, mais sans plus. Sous leurs pieds, s'étend une belle neige pure et lisse.

Non loin de là, dans la forêt, Bob Les Oreilles Bigras progresse péniblement. Il n'a pas chaussé de raquettes et il s'enfonce, à chaque pas, jusqu'aux genoux. Il tire quelque chose de lourd avec une corde qu'il a passée sur son épaule: un objet pas très gros, mais massif. Bob peste:

— Qu'est-ce qu'il faut pas faire pour ramasser un peu d'argent.

Il sourit.

— Pas mal d'argent... Il y a toujours quelqu'un qui est prêt à acheter ce qui est interdit. Et moi, Bob, je suis prêt à le vendre. Bon, ici, ça devrait aller.

Il défait le sac de toile et en sort un piège. Un piège dont l'usage est illégal. Il possède d'énormes dents en acier prêtes à se refermer sur la patte qui a le malheur de se poser dessus. L'animal n'a alors aucun moyen de se sauver. À moins de se ronger lui-même la patte avec ses dents.

De son côté, M. Leboeuf attend au téléphone depuis une bonne demi-heure. Il doit rester en ligne pour conserver sa priorité d'appel. L'état civil est débordé. L'appareil sans fil coincé entre l'épaule et l'oreille droite, il sert ses clients.

Quant à Jean É. Chassé, il pénètre à son tour dans les bois. Quelque peu ralenti par son attirail, il avance, tout heureux. Il chantonne:

— À nous deux, le loup! Tu vas avoir affaire à Ti-Loup!

***

— S'il y a un loup, il est probablement bien caché, soupire Jocelyne, qui, avec ses amis, se risque dans un bouquet de sapins.

— S'il y a un loup, il va nécessairement sentir le beau morceau de viande dans le piège, se dit Bob, déjà triomphant.

— Si je le savais, je ne vous demanderais pas de chercher! rugit M. Leboeuf dans le téléphone.

— Si le soleil est dans cette position, c'est que le nord est par là, en déduit Jean É. Chassé, qui part vers l'est.

En haut d'une butte, des yeux observent. «Si tous ces gens sont ici, c'est pour moi.»

Chapitre VI
Quand on parle du loup, on lui voit le bout... de la patte

Au milieu de l'après-midi, le soleil commence déjà à décliner. Bientôt, il est si bas que l'ombre projetée par les trois inséparables s'étire loin devant eux.

Ils n'ont rien vu, rien aperçu. Notdog a bien débusqué un lièvre et jappé après un chevreuil, mais il n'a pas flairé la moindre odeur suspecte ni découvert la plus petite trace de loup.

Jocelyne, Agnès et John ont donc rebroussé chemin. Le froid leur a rougi les joues et s'empare de leurs orteils.

Bob Les Oreilles Bigras a abandonné son piège depuis longtemps, en se disant: «Si le loup se prend la patte là-dedans, il ne pourra pas se sauver, alors pourquoi me faire geler les rotules à l'attendre? Je vais aller niaiser au chaud chez Steve La Patate, en attendant de retourner voir plus tard.»

M. Leboeuf est rivé à son téléphone et attend que l'état civil le rappelle.

Jean É. Chassé regarde le soleil se coucher et décide de rentrer. «Le soleil se couche à l'ouest, alors je retourne de ce côté», pense-t-il.

Le clocher de l'église est en vue, lorsque les inséparables entendent le hurlement.

Un hurlement à glacer le sang.

Un hurlement de douleur.

Agnès est la première à réagir:

— Qu'est-ce qu'on fait? On est encore loin! On va être attaqués! lance-t-elle, prise de panique.

— On n'a pas le choix: on court le plus vite qu'on peut! décide Jocelyne, qui s'élance déjà, suivie d'Agnès, en direction du village.

John ne bouge pas.

— Qu'est-ce que tu fais? demande Agnès.

— Je...

Le hurlement.

— Je crois qu'on devrait aller voir. Ça ne vient pas de loin.

— T'es malade!? s'écrie Jocelyne.

— Non. Nous sommes trois, il ne va pas nous attaquer! Et puis, je trouve que ça ressemble à une plaine.

— À une plainte, tu veux dire? le corrige Agnès.

— Oui.

Notdog, qui attendait sagement que les enfants veuillent bien se décider pour les suivre, se met tout à coup à flairer le vent. Il fait quelques pas, renifle encore et émet alors des grognements sourds.

— Qu'est-ce que tu as? demande Jocelyne.

Notdog s'impatiente, grogne, jappe, avance, recule.

— Qu'est-ce que tu sens? Pas le loup, j'espère, s'inquiète sa maîtresse.

Notdog fait quelques pas en direction du bois, hésite, comme s'il ne voulait pas y aller. Mais il s'élance finalement, poussé par l'instinct ou la curiosité.

51

Est-ce aussi l'instinct et la curiosité, ou bien le courage, la folie, même, qui s'emparent des inséparables? Peut-être un mélange de tout ça les fait suivre Notdog.

Ils ne marchent pas longtemps avant de l'apercevoir: un loup magnifique, au pelage gris et roux. Ses yeux jaunes et perçants les fixent. Son regard est-il menaçant? Ou implorant? Il ne bouge pas. Il ne peut pas. Il a la patte de devant gauche prise dans le piège installé par Bob.

Les inséparables s'approchent lentement. Notdog grogne. Le loup gémit de douleur.

Les enfants s'arrêtent à bonne distance.

— Il faut le libérer, dit John.

— D'accord, mais comment? C'est toi qui vas aller ouvrir le piège, je suppose? se moque Jocelyne.

— Oui, répond John.

— Écoute, c'est dangereux. En plus, le loup est blessé. On ne sait pas comment il va réagir. Et s'il te sautait dessus dès que tu l'auras libéré? Il faut aller chercher de l'aide, insiste Agnès.

— Pour qu'on le capture? Jamais!

John n'écoute plus personne et marche prudemment vers le piège en regardant la

bête droit dans les yeux. Elle l'observe, s'assoit, cesse de gémir. John lui parle tout doucement:

— Il ne faut pas avoir peur de moi. Je ne veux pas te faire de mal. Je veux juste te libérer de ça. Comprends-tu?

L'animal reste immobile.

John détache ses raquettes et va les coincer dans le piège pour éviter qu'il se referme. Il regarde le loup dans les yeux, lui répète d'une voix calme de ne pas avoir peur. Il lui explique qu'il va maintenant ouvrir le piège.

De toutes ses forces il écarte les dents meurtrières. L'animal fait un bond de côté, et le piège se referme sur les raquettes qui cassent en plusieurs morceaux sous l'énorme pression.

Pendant quelques secondes, rien ne bouge. Jocelyne tient son chien pour l'empêcher de sauter sur le loup et de peut-être y laisser sa vie. Agnès retient son souffle. John, à genoux, tremble. L'animal fixe sur lui son regard sans expression. Puis, péniblement, il s'enfonce davantage dans la forêt protectrice.

Le soleil qui se couche éclaire à peine le rouge des gouttes de sang sur la neige.

C'est à ce moment que les inséparables re-
marquent la tuque oubliée par Bob.

***

Cette nuit-là, la jeune fille revient au
village. Mais cette fois-ci, elle ne va pas à
la boucherie. Elle marche en silence sous
la fenêtre de la chambre de John.

Elle s'arrête, lève les yeux vers la vitre
glacée. Mais John n'y apparaîtra pas. Car
il dort profondément.

Aux premières lueurs de l'aube, elle
quitte l'ombre qui la cachait pour sortir du
village. Seul un chien, le museau à peine
sorti de sa niche, jappe sur son passage.

Chapitre VII
Telle mère, telle fille

À dix heures ce mardi matin, le thermomètre marque moins vingt-deux degrés. Le système de chauffage n'est pas encore réparé: l'école reste fermée aujourd'hui. Dans toutes les maisons, les gens se plaignent du froid et se demandent comment ils font pour vivre dans un pays pareil.

Le seul que la situation ravit est Joe, du garage Joe Auto. Car depuis trois jours, il est fort occupé à survolter toutes les voitures qui ne veulent pas démarrer. Et il y en a beaucoup.

Les inséparables viennent de se retrouver chez Agnès, autour d'un chocolat chaud. Sa mère fait les meilleurs du village, car elle fait fondre pas une mais deux guimauves dans chaque tasse.

Ils aimeraient bien raconter leur aventure, dénoncer Bob Les Oreilles Bigras et son piège illégal, mais voilà: si les parents apprennent l'affaire, ils savent qu'ils ne pourront plus sortir. Pour une semaine au moins.

Agnès boit à petites gorgées, et le chocolat lui laisse une moustache brune sous le nez.

En même temps, ils feuillettent un livre sur les loups, que Jocelyne a déniché sur un présentoir à la tabagie de son oncle.

— Regardez celui-là en pleine course, dit-elle. La légende dit qu'un loup peut atteindre une vitesse de soixante-quatre kilomètres à l'heure et qu'il peut courir longtemps avant de se fatiguer.

John se lèche les babines:

— Celui-ci ressemble au nôtre. C'est écrit que le loup a l'ouïe si fine qu'il peut déceler des sons à plus de dix kilomètres de distance.

Jocelyne tend sa tasse à Notdog. «Miam, par ici le chocolat, pense-t-il. Il n'en restera pas une goutte!» De fait, Jocelyne reprend une tasse parfaitement propre.

Sauf pour l'odeur. Puis, elle remarque:

— Regardez! Ici on dit qu'un loup peut avaler jusqu'à neuf kilos de viande en une seule fois! Après, il peut rester deux semaines sans manger. Tiens, tiens... Neuf kilos... C'est la quantité de viande que la jeune fille mystérieuse a volée.

Agnès réfléchit tout haut:

— Tu crois qu'elle l'a volée pour un loup? Pour notre loup?

— C'est vrai que c'est une bizarre de cadence, dit John.

Agnès reprend:

— De coïncidence, John, pas de cadence.

C'est alors que la mère d'Agnès lui demande:

— J'ai besoin de viande pour mon pâté chinois. Irais-tu en chercher chez le boucher, s'il te plaît?

— Tout de suite, répond sa fille.

Et les voilà dehors en un rien de temps.

M. Leboeuf est seul dans son magasin. Lorsqu'il voit entrer les enfants, il sourit:

— Ah! enfin des clients!

— Vous n'êtes pas trop occupé, on dirait, lance Agnès.

— Ma foi, je crois que le froid a rendu tout le monde végétarien. Vous désirez?

— Un kilo de steak haché maigre, s'il vous plaît.

Le boucher ouvre la porte de son comptoir réfrigéré et plonge une large cuillère dans une montagne de viande:

— Si ça continue comme ça, je vais perdre tout mon stock.

Jocelyne pousse John du coude. Il hésite, s'éclaircit la voix:

— Euh, c'est au sujet de la jeune fille qui vous a volé la viande...

Surpris, le boucher échappe sa cuillère:

— Co... comment, que... quelle jeune fille? bredouille-t-il.

— Celle qu'on voit sur la cassette, répond Jocelyne.

Il bondit vers eux:

— La cassette, vous avez retrouvé la cassette?

Agnès répond:

— Dans votre poubelle. Notdog l'a trouvée, et nous l'avons regardée. On voit très bien une jeune fille voler une énorme quantité de viande.

— Vous l'avez toujours? Je veux dire, la cassette? demande M. Leboeuf, inquiet.

Les enfants font signe que oui.

— Merci mon Dieu! J'étais tellement énervé que j'ai dû la jeter sans m'en rendre compte. Je me souviens très bien de l'avoir déposée sur le comptoir, à côté des boîtes vides, et probablement qu'en les jetant, j'ai pris la cassette et...

Jocelyne lui coupe la parole:

— Pourquoi avoir dit qu'on ne voyait rien sur le vidéo, l'autre jour, à la tabagie?

Le boucher s'essuie les mains sur une

61

serviette déjà rouge de sang. Il soupire:

— Je suis si peu sûr de moi... J'ai cru reconnaître quelqu'un et j'ai voulu vérifier son identité.

— Qui? demande John.

— Ça ne sert à rien de conter des blagues, j'imagine.

Le boucher s'appuie sur le comptoir, met les mains dans ses poches, cherche ses mots. Puis, il raconte:

— Il y a dix-sept ans, une femme, qui se nommait Agathe, est disparue. Malgré les recherches, les battues, les chiens policiers entraînés, on ne l'a jamais retrouvée. Je suis même la dernière personne à l'avoir vue. C'était la nuit, et je ne m'endormais pas. Je regardais dehors et j'ai vu Agathe. Elle marchait dans la rue avec un inconnu. Il faisait très noir, et je n'ai pas pu distinguer l'homme. On ne les a jamais revus, ni l'un ni l'autre.

Le boucher s'arrête.

— Quel est le rapport avec la jeune fille? Elle n'a certainement pas plus de seize ans, remarque Agnès.

— Elle est le sosie d'Agathe. À part ses yeux bizarres, c'est son portrait vivant. Vous comprenez, j'ai pensé que c'était

peut-être sa fille. Et que... peut-être qu'Agathe est toujours en vie...

En voyant l'air si triste de M. Leboeuf, Jocelyne comprend bien des choses:

— Vous aimiez beaucoup Agathe.

— C'était ma fiancée.

Gêné, le boucher regarde ses grosses mains rouges. Doucement, Jocelyne lui demande:

— Mais pourquoi avoir menti?

— Parce que je voulais être sûr de moi.

Je ne voulais pas qu'on dise que j'imagine des choses. Le fait est que la jeune fille n'est pas revenue. Je ne la reverrai peut-être jamais.

John avoue:

— Moi, je l'ai vue aussi.

Les yeux du boucher s'illuminent:

— Quand? Où?

C'est alors que la porte s'ouvre. Bob Les Oreilles Bigras entre, visiblement de très mauvaise humeur:

— De la viande, boucher, la moins chère à part de ça.

John, qui aimerait bien lui sauter à la figure, ne peut s'empêcher de lui lancer:

— Si tu espères attirer un autre animal dans ton piège, oublie ça! On s'en va à la police te démancher!

— Dénoncer, John, pas démancher, le reprend Agnès qui, à son tour, regarde Bob d'un air de défi.

Mais Bob fait l'innocent:

— Un piège? Quel piège? Moi!? Attraper un pauvre animal au piège! Voyons donc! Je ne ferais pas de mal à une mouche, à moins qu'elle me pique.

— Laisse faire! On sait que c'est toi. On a trouvé ta tuque, dit Jocelyne, oubliant les parents.

— Je ne porte jamais de tuque, c'est trop laid! ment Bob.

C'est alors que la porte s'ouvre de nouveau. Le chef de police entre, tout essoufflé:

— M. Leboeuf, on a besoin de vous pour une battue. Jean É. Chassé n'est pas rentré, hier. Il est certainement perdu en forêt.

Le boucher enfile déjà ses bottes:

— Mon Dieu! J'espère qu'il n'est pas déjà mort gelé!

Bob profite de l'inattention des autres pour se glisser dehors. Il se sauve en marmonnant:

— Vous allez me le payer, sales microbes.

Chapitre VIII

La vengeance est un plat qui se mange très, très, très froid

Les inséparables ont décidé de filer en douce pour participer aux recherches. Mais le père de John, qui organise la battue, les a repérés et a immédiatement renvoyé son fils à la maison.

L'air de rien, Agnès, Jocelyne et Notdog se sont éloignés et ont pris la direction du bois.

De son côté, Jean É. Chassé vient de passer la nuit la plus longue de sa vie.

La veille, il a marché une bonne heure avant de se rendre compte qu'il avait fait fausse route. La nuit tombant, il ne pouvait continuer et il a dû admettre qu'il était bel et bien perdu. Dans un froid sibérien. Sans abri. Sans nourriture.

Heureusement, il avait des allumettes. Il a ramassé des brindilles sèches et de petites branches, et a réussi à allumer un feu malgré le vent. Il s'y est collé toute la nuit, luttant contre le sommeil pour ne pas risquer que le feu s'éteigne.

Au matin, il a repris sa route en se disant qu'il aurait dû prendre le temps de trouver sa boussole. Il a marché, marché, sans savoir où il se trouvait.

Au village, toutes les personnes valides sont parties à la recherche de l'expert du ministère de la Faune.

John marche lentement vers la tabagie. Il va y acheter un billet de loto, pour sa mère.

Il regarde par terre, s'ennuie. Tout à coup, il entend près de lui un souffle. Il fige. Puis se retourne. Devant lui, Bob Les Oreilles Bigras arbore son plus méchant sourire.

— Alors, c'est à toi, la raquette en morceaux?

— Oui, et après?

— On s'amuse à mettre ses raquettes dans les affaires des autres, hum?

— Tu n'avais pas le droit de capturer le loup!

— Ah, parce que c'était bien le loup que j'avais pris... Et où sont les deux sangsues qui collent toujours après toi?

Pour toute réponse, John hausse les épaules et se retourne pour continuer son chemin. Bob l'agrippe par le foulard:

— Pas si vite. On a des comptes à régler.

— Lâche-moi! crie John.

Mais Bob lui met une main devant la bouche et le serre très fort de l'autre bras, de sorte que John n'a pas d'autre choix que de le suivre.

Bob l'entraîne non loin de là, dans une remise délabrée.

— Alors, j'ai perdu mon loup. Ça mérite une petite leçon. Qu'est-ce que tu dirais de rester prisonnier ici jusqu'à ce que tu aies si froid qu'un de tes orteils tombe? Un orteil pour un loup, c'est juste.

Bob s'aperçoit soudain que John ne le regarde plus. Le garçon observe intensément quelque chose derrière lui.

— Heille! Regarde-moi quand je te

parle, microbe.

Comme John ne lui obéit pas, Bob se retourne. Dans l'embrasure de la porte, un loup le fixe de ses yeux dorés.

L'animal avance lentement, montrant les crocs.

Pris de panique, Bob s'élance à travers une fenêtre en brisant les carreaux. On l'entend crier:

— Ayoye donc!

Puis il disparaît.

Paralysé par la peur, John peut à peine respirer. Le loup est devant lui. Le garçon tourne les yeux vers la fenêtre par laquelle s'est enfui Bob et se demande comment il pourrait faire pour s'y jeter lui-même. Il entend alors une voix douce:

— N'aie pas peur. Je ne te veux pas de mal.

Il regarde devant lui. La jeune voleuse de viande est là.

Chapitre IX
Un loup
déguisé en brebis

La jeune fille sourit. Elle s'approche de John. Elle porte un manteau de fourrure gris et roux. Ses yeux ont un étrange reflet doré.

Ébranlé, timide, émerveillé devant la grande beauté de la jeune fille, John cherche quelque chose à dire... et le loup, qui a disparu.

— Mais où est le loup? demande-t-il.

— Il est ici, répond-elle.

— Tu es sa maîtresse? Tu l'as approuvé?

La jeune fille fronce les sourcils:

— Approuvé?

— Je veux dire, il t'obéit?

— Ah! Apprivoisé. C'est un peu ça.

C'est plus que ça.

Elle semble hésiter. Puis, elle poursuit:

— Tu n'as pas eu peur de lui. Tu l'as libéré de son piège. Il te doit la vie.

Elle prend la main de John dans les siennes tout emmitouflées:

— Je ne te remercierai jamais assez.

John baisse les yeux et il remarque les poignets de la jeune fille, qui se sont dénudés lorsqu'elle a tendu les mains. Le gauche est enveloppé dans un bout de tissu imprégné de sang.

— Qu'est-ce qui t'est arrivé? demande John.

La jeune fille ne répond pas. Elle réfléchit. Puis, elle ajoute:

— Je vais te révéler un secret. Je ne veux pas que tu aies peur.

— Peur? Et pourquoi j'aurais peur?

— Regarde.

La jeune fille recule. Elle ferme les yeux, tombe à quatre pattes, et en quelques secondes celle qui lui tenait les mains a pris la forme d'un loup. D'un vrai. La forme de celui qu'il a libéré du piège et qui l'a délivré à son tour de Bob Les Oreilles Bigras.

C'est alors que John remarque le bandage sur la patte de devant gauche. Il a dit qu'il n'aurait pas peur. Mais tous ses membres se mettent à trembler en même temps et ses dents à claquer sans qu'il puisse s'en empêcher.

Il assiste alors à une nouvelle transformation. L'animal se lève sur les pattes de derrière, son museau s'aplatit, le poil des joues disparaît, et la jeune fille réapparaît:

— Je t'en prie, n'aie pas peur.

— C'est de la magie? arrive-t-il à articuler.

— Non.

— Tu es... tu es... un loup? Un vrai loup?

— Oui. Je vais tout t'expliquer. Viens.

Elle s'avance pour prendre la main de John qui, machinalement, la retire. Il rit, puis la lui tend. Ils s'improvisent des sièges avec une chaise défoncée et un vieux pupitre.

Elle s'assoit face à John et fixe sur lui ses yeux de loup, brillants, froids. Devant ce regard, il ne peut s'empêcher d'avoir un frisson dans le dos. N'est-elle pas une bête avec tout ce que cela implique de réactions imprévisibles?

Mais sa voix se fait rassurante:

— Il y a près de dix-sept ans, mon père, un loup, est tombé amoureux d'une femme, ma mère. Mais pour l'approcher, il lui fallait être un homme. Et il l'est devenu. Pour un temps.

— Comment?

— C'est l'esprit de la forêt qui l'a aidé. Cela fait partie de tous ces secrets de la nature, dont les humains ne soupçonnent même pas l'existence.

«Mon père est donc devenu un homme, droit, fier, fort. Il a gagné le coeur de ma mère, qui est partie avec lui. Je suis née un an plus tard, petite fille moitié louve moitié humaine.

«Je ne me souviens pas de ma mère, car elle est morte quand j'étais bébé. Alors, mon père est redevenu un loup, et j'ai été élevée comme un loup. Après tout, j'en suis un.»

John avait presque oublié ce détail, et un autre frisson lui parcourt la colonne vertébrale. Mais il a mille questions à poser à cette étrange créature tout droit sortie d'une légende.

— Tu vivais avec une bande de loups?

— Non, avec mon père.

— Où est-il?

— Il est mort de vieillesse, il y a trois mois. Les loups ne vivent pas très vieux, treize, quatorze ans normalement.

— Mais toi, quel âge as-tu?

— Moi, je suis à moitié humaine, je vivrai plus longtemps. J'ai quinze ans.

— Tu as mangé toute la viande que tu as volée?

La jeune fille éclate de rire:

— Mais oui.

— Dis-moi, tu as un nom? Moi, c'est John.

— Et moi, Agathe.

— C'est le nom de ta mère.

Pour la première fois, la jeune fille perd son flegme. John perçoit l'émotion vive qui envahit la louve lorsqu'elle demande:

— Comment le sais-tu?

John lui raconte l'histoire du boucher et de sa ressemblance avec la fiancée de M. Leboeuf. Il finit en suggérant:

— Peut-être a-t-il des photos d'elle?

Agathe se lève, marche en long et en large. Ah! voir sa mère! Cette possibilité la rend fébrile. Ce que John a devant lui, c'est une jeune fille agile, souple et agitée comme un animal sauvage.

Il regrette presque ses paroles. Il est

inquiet. Agathe tourne en rond et gémit comme un chiot: le son n'a rien d'humain. Elle s'arrête:

— John, pourras-tu m'aider?

— À faire quoi?

— Je voudrais que tu demandes à M. Leboeuf si, effectivement, il a des photos ou quelque chose qui a appartenu à ma mère et que tu me l'apportes.

— Sans lui parler de toi, je suppose.

— Sans lui parler de moi.

— Je vais essayer. Maintenant, il est parti à la recherche de l'agent du ministère de la Faune, mais demain... Il faut que tu me laisses jusqu'à demain, oui. Tu pourras revenir?

— Demain. Je ne sais pas.

— Pourquoi?

— À minuit ce soir, j'aurai seize ans.

— Et alors?

Agathe se fait grave:

— Il me reste jusqu'à minuit ce soir pour décider ce que je veux être: un humain ou un loup. Ainsi en a décidé l'esprit de la forêt. Après, je ne pourrai plus jamais être autre chose que ce que j'aurai choisi.

— Tu ne le sais pas encore? s'étonne John.

Du dehors leur parviennent des voix d'hommes:

— À cette heure-ci, il est sûrement mort gelé.

— Tu trouveras l'homme que vous cherchez à exactement un kilomètre au nord du piège dont tu m'as libérée. Suivez le ruisseau jusqu'au grand chêne. Il n'y en a qu'un, dit Agathe, qui se métamorphose en louve.

— Attends! lui crie John.

Mais elle est déjà partie.

Chapitre X
Le choix d'Agathe

Au tournant de la rue, John voit arriver ses amies. Notdog le rejoint en courant, puis le renifle avec insistance.

— On te cherchait partout. Où étais-tu? s'exclame Agnès.

— Tu t'es roulé dans la viande? demande Jocelyne en voyant faire son chien.

— Vous avez trouvé Jean É. Chassé? s'enquiert John.

Agnès se mouche dans ses mitaines avant de répondre:

— Non. C'est dramatique. Il va mourir, si ce n'est pas déjà fait. Nous, on est revenues parce qu'on est complètement gelées. Mais qu'est-ce que tu fais ici?

— Il ne faut pas perdre une minute. Je

sais où trouver Chassé. Venez, dit John.

— Eh! Attends. Comment ça se fait que tu sais ça? demande Jocelyne.

— Je vais vous expliquer en marchant. Venez.

En filant vers la forêt, John raconte à ses amies incrédules l'histoire d'Agathe, ses transformations, le choix qu'elle doit faire. Ensemble, ils cherchent un moyen d'obtenir une photo de la mère d'Agathe, sans tout révéler à M. Leboeuf, puisque Agathe ne le veut pas.

— Peut-être qu'il faudrait au contraire tout lui dire, suggère Jocelyne. Après tout, c'était sa fiancée.

Rendu au piège de Bob, John fait part de son opinion:

— Pour l'instant, je ne pense pas que ce serait une bonne chose de le mettre au comptant.

— Au courant, tu veux dire, le reprend Agnès. Pourquoi?

— Parce qu'il faut laisser à Agathe le temps de prendre sa décision. Si elle choisit d'être humaine, on lui demandera si elle est d'accord pour tout dire au boucher. Il pourra peut-être s'occuper d'elle.

— Et si elle préfère rester un loup...

commence Agnès.

— M. Leboeuf est un adulte. Il partira à sa recherche et ne la laissera pas tranquille, dit John.

— Pour ça, il faudrait qu'il nous croie! remarque Agnès, toujours pratique.

Jocelyne, très sensible aux émotions des gens, murmure:

— Il est si bouleversé que je pense qu'il est prêt à croire n'importe quoi pour la retrouver... Dis, John, quel choix fera-t-elle, tu penses?

Pour toute réponse, John hausse les épaules. Il ne sait vraiment pas.

Une demi-heure plus tard, Notdog bondit en avant, aboyant. Ils le suivent et trouvent Jean É. Chassé, étendu dans la neige, exactement à l'endroit indiqué par Agathe. Agnès se penche sur lui:

— Il respire encore.

***

John est retourné au village chercher de l'aide. À l'auberge, on a tout simplement téléphoné au chef de police, qui traîne toujours son cellulaire, et les secours sont arrivés à toute vitesse.

Jean É. Chassé a été rapidement transporté à l'auberge. Il en sera quitte pour perdre ses deux petits orteils. En attendant l'ambulance qui le conduira à l'hôpital, il raconte qu'il a vu le loup, immense, tout blanc et menaçant.

Agnès et Jocelyne savent bien qu'il ment, car le loup n'est pas blanc. L'expert raconte des histoires... de chasse.

— À sa place, j'irais travailler dans un zoo, dit Agnès. Là il en verrait pour de vrai, des loups.

M. Leboeuf s'approche d'elles:

— Vraiment, les enfants, vous êtes des héros! Quel flair! Des chasseurs-nés! J'espère que ce monsieur n'oubliera jamais qu'il vous doit la vie. Mais, au fait, où est John? Il n'a pas eu le temps de me dire où il a vu la jeune fille, et je...

Jocelyne bafouille:

— Euh, il est parti, il est parti... chez lui, oui, ses vêtements étaient mouillés, il est allé se changer.

— Je devrais faire la même chose, rentrer chez moi, dit l'homme.

— Non, non, non! Je peux vous dire, moi, où il a vu la jeune fille, commence Agnès, qui doit retenir le boucher pendant que John fouille sa maison.

Il cherche une photo. La photo d'une femme qui ressemble à Agathe. Il ouvre des tiroirs, des armoires. Sur une tablette, dans la garde-robe, il découvre une boîte. Il l'ouvre. Il y trouve des photos, certaines très anciennes. Des photos d'un petit garçon — le boucher —, des photos de famille, des photos d'inconnus.

Tout au fond, dans une grande enveloppe brune, un portrait. John sait tout de suite que c'est elle. Il remet la photo dans l'enveloppe, la cache sous son manteau et sort.

Il frappe dans la grande fenêtre en saillie de l'auberge. Agnès et Jocelyne s'habillent en vitesse et sortent discrètement.

***

Dans la remise, John, Agnès et Jocelyne attendent. Notdog aussi attend, mais il ne sait pas quoi. «Si on est pour rien faire, on devrait au moins le faire au chaud», pense-t-il, roulé en boule pour garder sa chaleur.

Dehors, la fin de l'après-midi amène la noirceur. Tout disparaît rapidement dans la nuit.

La pleine lune se lève. Les inséparables ne disent pas un mot. John est fébrile, Agnès et Jocelyne tout de même un peu inquiètes.

— Il va falloir rentrer, ma mère va me chercher, dit Agnès.

— Mon oncle aussi, enchaîne Jocclyne.

— Moi, je reste, décide John.

Les filles vont attendre encore dix minutes. Après neuf minutes, c'est Notdog qui l'entend venir le premier. Il grogne, et Jocelyne agrippe son chien. Chacun retient son souffle. Et dans un rayon de lune apparaît la jeune fille.

Elle hésite à entrer.

— N'aie pas peur, elles ne te feront aucun mal.

Agathe entre, mais s'arrête près de la porte, prudente comme une louve qu'elle est. John s'approche. Il lui tend l'enveloppe brune.

— Voilà. Une photo de ta mère.

Agathe ouvre l'enveloppe et regarde. C'est la première fois qu'elle voit sa mère. Ses yeux s'emplissent de larmes. Elle serre la photo sur son coeur, l'examine à nouveau.

— Elle a l'air douce, elle est si belle.

Merci à vous.

— Agathe... Qu'est-ce que tu vas décider? lui demande John.

— Je ne sais pas encore. Il y a la nature, la droiture, la liberté d'un côté; l'inconnu de l'autre.

— Tu sais, nous sommes là... Je suis là, finit par dire John, qu'une émotion trop grande envahit.

Agathe lui sourit, et pour la première fois ses yeux dorés toujours si froids s'imprègnent d'une grande tendresse. Elle lui caresse la joue et sort dans la nuit.

**

John s'est posté à la fenêtre de sa chambre et a guetté Agathe toute la nuit, sans la voir. Il s'est endormi, appuyé aux carreaux. Le lendemain, le mercure a monté, au grand bonheur de tous. En se levant, John apprend par sa mère que l'école rouvrira dès le lendemain. Il refuse les rôties qu'elle lui tend et sort à toute vitesse.

Il scrute le paysage, puis fait le tour de la maison, cherchant un signe d'Agathe. Il le trouve sous sa fenêtre. Des traces de pas font battre son coeur. Mais bientôt, les

traces deviennent celles d'un loup et elles
se perdent en direction de la forêt.

Chapitre XI

Il n'y a qu'une vie à vivre, et c'est en bande que je veux la vivre

Elles l'ont trouvé près du piège de Bob. John tournait en rond, tristement. Il ne les a même pas entendues venir. De fait, c'est Notdog qui a signalé leur présence en sautant sur John, pour jouer.

— Alors? lance Jocelyne, fébrile.

— Tu l'as vue? demande à son tour Agnès.

Mais à l'air de John, elles comprennent vite. Il ne se lance pas dans de longues explications. Quelques mots seulement suffisent:

— Des traces sous ma fenêtre... des traces de... loup.

Ils marchent un moment dans la neige rendue collante par le redoux. Puis, John casse une branche de pin séchée et la lance de toutes ses forces dans un ruisseau coulant en cascade.

— Je ne comprends pas pourquoi elle a choisi de devenir un loup, dit-il avec colère.

— C'est ce qu'elle a toujours connu, suggère Jocelyne.

— C'est son monde, sa vraie famille, continue Agnès.

John n'est pas convaincu.

— Mais elle a parlé de droiture, de nature, de liberté; est-ce que ça n'existe pas aussi pour les humains?

Ni Jocelyne ni Agnès n'ont de réponse à cette question.

Au retour, elles racontent que Bob a disparu du village. Sûrement parce qu'il a eu la peur de sa vie!

Elles parlent aussi de M. Leboeuf. Les inséparables décident qu'ils ne lui diront rien d'Agathe, puisqu'elle n'existe plus. En tant que personne. Avec un peu de chance, le boucher ne s'apercevra jamais

que la photo au fond de sa boîte a disparu, emportée par un loup.

Agnès parle ensuite de l'école, qui reprend le lendemain. Jocelyne a de la difficulté à garder secrètes les choses extraordinaires qu'ils ont vécues ces derniers jours.

— On pourra peut-être en faire une histoire... Enfin, un jour, si un de nous devient écrivain, dit-elle.

Silencieux, John écoute ses grandes amies. Et il se sent soudain tout heureux de les avoir avec lui.

— On sera toujours les irremplaçables, O.K.?

— Les inséparables, le reprend Agnès tendrement.

— Les irremplaçables aussi, ajoute Jocelyne en souriant.

Ils rentrent au village en se lançant des balles de neige, en courant et en riant.

Tout près, une louve les regarde s'en aller. Puis, elle prend la direction du nord, à la recherche d'une bande de loups qui deviendra sa nouvelle famille.

Table des matières

Achevé d'imprimer
sur les presses de Litho Acme inc.

CONTENTS

The New Testament 57

GOSPELS & ACTS   59

THE OLD TESTAMENT

Books of the Old Testament

The Old Testament is made up of thirty-nine books, divided into four main sections.

PENTATEUCH	HISTORICAL BOOKS	POETRY & WISDOM BOOKS
Genesis	Joshua	Job
Exodus	Judges	Psalms
Leviticus	Ruth	Proverbs
Numbers	1 Samuel	Ecclesiastes
Deuteronomy	2 Samuel	Song of Songs
	1 Kings	
	2 Kings	
	1 Chronicles	
	2 Chronicles	
	Ezra	
	Nehemiah	
	Esther	

PROPHETIC BOOKS		
Major Prophets:	*Minor Prophets:*	
Isaiah	Hosea	Nahum
Jeremiah	Joel	Habakkuk
Lamentations	Amos	Zephaniah
Ezekiel	Obadiah	Haggai
Daniel	Jonah	Zechariah
	Micah	Malachi

PENTATEUCH

What Is the Pentateuch?

The Pentateuch is the first five books of the Bible: Genesis, Exodus, Leviticus, Numbers, and Deuteronomy.

- The word *Pentateuch* comes from a Greek word that means "five scrolls."
- In Hebrew, these books are known as the Torah, which means "law" or "instruction."
- It is God's instructions for a nation learning to be God's people.

These five books lay the basis for the rest of the Bible. They explain:

- The origin of the universe, of the nations, and of God's people.
- The need for God's direct intervention in human history—human sin.
- How God acts in the lives of his people.

Main Characters

- ***God:*** God is the Pentateuch's central focus. Each story reveals something about God, his character, or how he works.
- ***Abraham:*** Abraham's calling shows God's initiative to rescue humanity from sin and death.
- ***Israel:*** God decided to work his plan of salvation in and through Israel, a chosen people.
- ***Moses:*** Moses' life was bound to the life of God's people and to God himself.
- ***The Promised Land:*** The land is the concrete representation of God's promises to Abraham. The Israelites' relationship with the land becomes a constant theme in the Pentateuch and beyond.

BOOK	FOCUS
GENESIS	■ Origins of the world ■ Origins of the nations ■ Origins of God's people
EXODUS	■ God's people and their origin as a nation ■ Organizing the Israelites to become God's people
LEVITICUS	■ Equipping the people to become God's holy nation ■ The heart of the Torah (Pentateuch) is holiness
NUMBERS	■ Organization of God's people as God's army ■ On the way to reclaim the Promised Land ■ Death of the old generation ■ Birth of the new generation
DEUTERONOMY	■ God's instructions for a new generation ■ God's instructions for a generation at the entrance of the Promised Land ■ Basing the identity of God's people on the covenant

Ancient Middle East

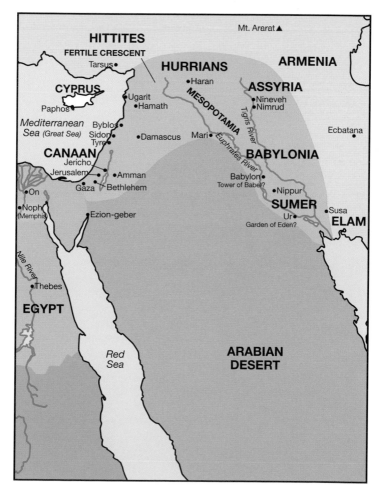

Mt. Ararat ▲

HITTITES
FERTILE CRESCENT
Tarsus•
HURRIANS
ARMENIA
CYPRUS
•Haran
ASSYRIA
Paphos•
•Ugarit
•Hamath
•Nineveh
•Nimrud
MESOPOTAMIA
Tigris River
Ecbatana •
Mediterranean
Sea (Great Sea)
Byblos•
Sidon•
Tyre•
•Damascus
Mari•
Euphrates River
BABYLONIA
CANAAN
Jericho•
Jerusalem•
•Amman
Babylon•
Tower of Babel?
•On
•Gaza
•Bethlehem
•Nippur
SUMER
•Noph
(Memphis)
•Ezion-geber
Ur•
Garden of Eden?
•Susa
ELAM
Nile River
•Thebes
EGYPT
Red
Sea
ARABIAN
DESERT

GENESIS

THE BEGINNINGS OF CREATION, THE NATIONS, AND THE ISRAELITES

WRITTEN c. 1446–1406 BC by Moses

PURPOSE To show that God is sovereign and loves his creation.

SUMMARY The book of Genesis is a book of origins: the good creation of the world, the start of human problems, and the beginning of God's solution to those problems. The stories in Genesis reveal deeply broken relationships: separation between God and his creation; rivalries among family members; and violence between people groups. Yet we also see God beginning to restore the brokenness by choosing a family—Abraham's family—and guiding and rescuing them along the way.

OUTLINE
- The beginning of the world (1–2)
- The beginning of nations (3–10)
- The beginning of the Israelites (11–50)

JESUS IN GENESIS As a book of origins, Genesis shows the origin of humanity's greatest predicament: sin. It also shows that God's mercy promised his own solution to this quandary: "And I will put enmity between you and the woman, and between your offspring and hers; he will crush your head, and you will strike his heel" (Genesis 3:15). God's promises in Genesis point to his final and perfect solution for humanity's fallen state: Jesus, God's own Son.

KEY VERSE
The Lord said to Abraham: *"I will establish my covenant as an everlasting covenant between me and you and your descendants."*
—Genesis 17:7

EXODUS

GOD'S DELIVERANCE OF THE ISRAELITES FROM SLAVERY IN EGYPT

WRITTEN c. 1446–1406 BC by Moses

PURPOSE To show God's faithfulness to the covenant and provide Israel with guidelines for holy living.

SUMMARY The book of Exodus tells the story of God's people moving from bondage to freedom. God chooses a man named Moses to lead the Israelites (Hebrews) out of slavery in Egypt and into the wilderness where they can worship God. The God of Israel proves himself to be the only true God, defeating the false gods of Egypt. At Mt. Sinai, God gives his people instructions on how to live as a community of holy people.

OUTLINE
- Israel in Egypt (1–15)
- Israel on the way toward Sinai (15–18)
- Israel at Sinai (19–40)

JESUS IN EXODUS Moses' ministry as judge, priest, and prophet anticipated Jesus' own ministry (Hebrews 3:1–6). The Passover celebration and sacrifice (Exodus 12) help us understand Christ's sacrifice on the cross on our behalf. In the exodus, God liberated Israel from the bondage of Pharaoh with great acts of power. Now, God has freed us from the bondage of sin and death with the greatest act of grace and power: Jesus' death and resurrection.

KEY VERSE
"God said to Moses, 'I AM WHO I AM.' This is what you are to say to the Israelites: 'I AM has sent me to you.'" —Exodus 3:14

LEVITICUS
LAW AND SACRIFICE

WRITTEN c. 1446–1406 BC by Moses

PURPOSE To instruct Israel on how to be holy and be a blessing to others.

SUMMARY The book of Leviticus teaches the Israelites how to live in the presence of a holy God. It is a detailed list of instructions for priests, purity rituals, and how to make atonement for the people's sins. The atonement made through sacrifices in Leviticus foreshadows Jesus' own sacrifice of himself on the cross that makes atonement for our sins today.

OUTLINE
- Sacrifice (1–7)
- Priesthood (8–10)
- Clean and unclean (11–15)
- Day of Atonement (16)
- Laws for daily life (17–27)

JESUS IN LEVITICUS God instructed his people from the tabernacle. The tabernacle, where God's presence dwelt, was the place of revelation. In it, God revealed his glory and his will for his people. Christ is God's perfect revelation (Hebrews 1:1–2; Colossians 1:15). Jesus himself came to the world as a human to "tabernacle" (dwell) among us (John 1:14) because he is God. Jesus fulfilled all the requirements of the law (Matthew 5:17), and he was the perfect sacrifice that makes all other sacrifices unnecessary (Hebrews 9:11–28).

KEY VERSE
"Consecrate yourselves and be holy, because I am the Lord your God." —Leviticus 20:7

NUMBERS

CENSUS AND HISTORY OF THE ISRAELITES IN THE WILDERNESS

WRITTEN c. 1446–1406 BC by Moses

PURPOSE To remind the people about the consequences of rebelling against God.

SUMMARY The book of Numbers is a story of rebellion and disobedience alongside God's grace and mercy. The book narrates the forty years the Israelites spent in the wilderness. God punishes his people when they rebel, but he preserves them and extends grace to the next generation who would enter the land he had promised to them.

OUTLINE
- First census and laws (1–9)
- Travels from Sinai to Canaan (10–12)
- The spies and the rebellion (13–25)
- Second census (26)
- Israelites in Moab (27–36)

JESUS IN NUMBERS God's grace extending to a new generation—an important theme in Numbers—is echoed in the New Testament. Just as Moses had characterized the generation of Israelites that died in the wilderness as "evil" (Deuteronomy 1:35), Jesus later characterized his generation as "wicked and adulterous" (Matthew 12:39; 16:4). And just as in Numbers, God's grace reached out to the following generation.

KEY VERSE
"The LORD bless you and keep you; the LORD make his face shine on you and be gracious to you." —Numbers 6:24–25

DEUTERONOMY

MOSES' FINAL SERMONS

WRITTEN c. 1446–1406 BC by Moses

PURPOSE To remind those who would enter the Promised Land what God expects from them.

SUMMARY After forty years in the wilderness, the people arrive in Moab at the border of the Promised Land. The book of Deuteronomy is a series of speeches Moses gave on the plains of Moab to challenge the younger generation to find their identity and purpose in their covenant with God.

OUTLINE
- Sermon 1: Journey Review (1–4)
- Sermon 2: Laws (5–28)
- Sermon 3: Covenant (29–30)
- Farewells and Moses' death (31–34)

JESUS IN DEUTERONOMY The glory to which we look forward will be revealed when Jesus returns. In the meantime, we continue to train and "press toward the goal to win the prize for which God has called me heavenward in Christ Jesus" (Philippians 3:14).

KEY VERSE
"Hear, O Israel: The LORD our God, the LORD is one. Love the LORD your God with all your heart and with all your soul and with all your strength." —Deuteronomy 6:4–5

HISTORICAL BOOKS

What Are the Historical Books?

These books (from Joshua to Esther) tell the story of the Israelites' historical experience with the Promised Land, with each other, and, most importantly, with their God.

This second section of the Bible picks up where the Pentateuch ends.

- Moses has died on Mt. Nebo, just outside the Promised Land.
- The Israelites are poised at the edge of the Promised Land.
- Joshua has been chosen to lead the people.

Major Events

The Historical Books cover the history of Israel from the time of the conquest (around the 1400s BC) to the time of Ezra and Nehemiah (around the 400s BC). In that time:

- Israel changed from a loosely organized group of 12 tribes to a united kingdom under David and Solomon.
- After King Solomon's death, the kingdom was divided in two: Israel in the north and Judah in the south.
- The Northern and Southern Kingdoms each had many kings who did evil in God's eyes. As punishment for Israel and Judah's disloyalty to God:
  - The Northern Kingdom was conquered by the Assyrians and forced into exile in 722 BC.
  - The Southern Kingdom was conquered by the Babylonians and forced into exile in 586 BC.

In the 400s BC, God restored a remnant of his people from Babylon. Ezra the priest and Nehemiah the governor returned with them. They reorganized the religious and political life of the people in Jerusalem.

JOSHUA

HISTORY OF THE CONQUEST OF THE PROMISED LAND

WRITTEN   c. 1300s BC by an unknown author (possibly Joshua or Samuel)

PURPOSE   To assure the people that obedience to God is rewarded.

SUMMARY   The book of Joshua is the story of how God brought his people into the land he had promised to them and gave them rest.

OUTLINE
- Conquest of the land (1–12)
- Dividing the land among the Israelite tribes (13–22)
- Joshua's farewell address (23–24)

JESUS IN JOSHUA   The name Joshua is connected to the Hebrew word *yehoshua*, which means "The Lord [Yahweh] is salvation," or "The Lord [Yahweh] gives victory." His initial name was Hoshea (Numbers 13:8, 16), which means "salvation." Moses changed his name to Joshua. The Greek form of the name Joshua is Jesus. Jesus is God's victory over sin and death. In Jesus, Christians are more than conquerors (Romans 8:37).

KEY VERSE
"Be strong and very courageous. Be careful to obey all the law my servant Moses gave you; do not turn from it to the right or to the left, that you may be successful wherever you go." —Joshua 1:7

JUDGES

CYCLES OF SIN AND DELIVERANCE IN THE PROMISED LAND

WRITTEN c. 1350–1000 BC by an unknown author (possibly Samuel)

PURPOSE To stress the importance of remaining loyal to God.

SUMMARY After the tribes of Israel settled in the Promised Land, they began a rapid moral and spiritual decline. But even in times when they turned their back to God and suffered the consequences, he was filled with compassion and mercy. When the people cried out to God, he raised up leaders (called judges) to deliver his people from oppression and usher in a period of peace. Yet after a while, the people would begin to do evil again, and the cycle would begin anew.

JESUS IN JUDGES The judges were deliverers God raised when they were needed. Jesus is God's solution to the problems of sin, oppression, suffering, and evil. His work is definite and final, though we are still waiting for the final fulfillment of God's promises.

OUTLINE
- Reasons for failure (1–2)
- The Judges (3–16)
- Days of lawlessness (17–21)

KEY VERSE
"In those days Israel had no king; everyone did as they saw fit."
—Judges 21:25

The Judges

JUDGE	REFERENCE	TRIBE	OPPRESSORS
OTHNIEL	3:7–11	Judah	Mesopotamians
EHUD	3:12–30	Benjamin	Moabites
SHAMGAR	3:31	Unknown	Philistines
DEBORAH	chapters 4–5	Ephraim	Canaanites
GIDEON	chapters 6–8	Manasseh	Midianites
TOLA	10:1–2	Issachar	Unknown
JAIR	10:3–5	Manasseh (Gilead)	Unknown
JEPHTHAH	10:6–12:7	Manasseh (Gilead)	Philistines and Ammonites
IBZAN	12:8–10	Judah	Unknown
ELON	12:11–12	Zebulun	Unknown
ABDON	12:13–15	Ephraim	Unknown
SAMSON	chapters 13–16	Dan	Philistines

RUTH

A STORY OF A FAITHFUL FOREIGNER

WRITTEN c. 1350–1000 BC by an unknown author (possibly Samuel)

PURPOSE To demonstrate the faithfulness and kindness that God desires for us.

SUMMARY Ruth's story is set during the era of judges, a time of moral and spiritual decay. Both Naomi (an Israelite) and her daughter-in-law Ruth (a Moabitess) become widowed and fall into poverty. Naomi returns from Moab to Bethlehem, and Ruth, in faithfulness to Naomi, goes with her, making Naomi's God her God. In Bethlehem, Ruth, "a woman of noble character" (3:11), meets Boaz, a man of kindness. Boaz, who is a relative of Naomi, accepts the role of guardian-redeemer, and marries Ruth and buys back Naomi's land.

OUTLINE
- Naomi returns to Bethlehem with Ruth (1)
- Ruth meets Boaz (2)
- Ruth seeks out Boaz to be the guardian-redeemer (3)
- Boaz marries Ruth (4)

JESUS IN RUTH The idea of a redeemer is important when we think of Jesus. Jesus redeems us from our fallen, low state. More directly, Ruth and Boaz are ancestors of Jesus our Savior—the ultimate guardian-redeemer (Matthew 1:5).

KEY VERSE
Ruth replied to Naomi, *"Your people will be my people and your God my God."* —Ruth 1:16

Characters in the Book of Ruth

NAME	MEANING	DESCRIPTION
ELIMELEK	"my God is king"	Husband of Naomi who moved his family from Bethlehem to Moab because of a famine. He died in Moab, leaving Naomi a widow.
NAOMI	"pleasant(ness)"	Elimelek's wife, who changed her name to Mara, meaning "bitterness," after her husband and sons died.
MAHLON	"tender" but also "sickly"	Son of Elimelek and Naomi. Married Ruth. Died in Moab.
KILION	"perfection" and also "destruction"	Son of Elimelek and Naomi. Married Orpah. Died in Moab.
ORPAH	"neck"	Wife of Kilion, the son of Naomi and Elimelek.
RUTH	"to befriend" and also "to comfort"	Although a Moabitess, Ruth became a "friend" of God's people, and a "comfort" to her mother-in-law, Naomi.
BOAZ	"in whom in strength"	Boaz surely demonstrated great strength of character and convictions to carry on another person's (Naomi's closer relative's) responsibility toward Naomi.
OBED	"servant" or "worshiper"	Obed was the son of Boaz and Ruth, father of Jesse, and grandfather of David.

1 & 2 SAMUEL

GOD IS KING, BUT WE WANT A HUMAN KING

WRITTEN   c. 1100–931 BC by an unknown author

PURPOSE
1 Samuel: To record how Israel got a king.
2 Samuel: To record King David's victories and failures.

SUMMARY
Named after Samuel—a prophet and Israel's last judge—the book of 1 Samuel shows God's hand in history during the transition from the judges through the reign of Israel's first king. God appoints King Saul, but eventually rejects him because he does not follow God's instructions. God then chooses a young shepherd named David to lead his people.

Second Samuel illustrates both God's blessing upon the faithful and the disastrous consequences of sin. Though chosen and blessed by God, King David forgets that God is the ultimate King. After David commits adultery with Bathsheba and murders her husband Uriah, family violence and national rebellion soon follow. Yet we also see God's mercy, as God forgives David when he repents.

OUTLINE

1 Samuel
- Samuel (1–7)
- Saul (8–15)
- David (16–31)

2 Samuel
- David's reign in Judah (1–4)
- David's reign over Israel (5–10)
- David's sin and family strife (11–24)

JESUS IN SAMUEL

Jesus is present in the book of Samuel in many different ways:

Samuel. His roles as prophet, judge, and priest anticipated Jesus' work during his earthly ministry.

Saul. Saul was God's answer to the people's request for a king. Saul's failure contrasts sharply with Jesus' victory: Jesus is God's answer to humanity's greatest need for a redeemer.

David. God's covenant with David anticipated the coming of a Messiah. This Messiah would unify God's people, bring true peace to the world, and bring God's kingdom to the whole earth.

The Hebrew Bible has only one book of Samuel. When the book was translated into Greek—the Septuagint—the translated text was significantly longer. To make it fit better in the scrolls, the translators of the Septuagint decided to break the book of Samuel into two parts. Originally, Samuel was called 1 and 2 books of Kings, and Kings was divided into 3 and 4 books of Kings.

KEY VERSES

Samuel replied to Saul: *"Does the LORD delight in burnt offerings and sacrifices as much as in obeying the LORD? To obey is better than sacrifice."* —1 Samuel 15:22

God's promise to David: *"I have been with you wherever you have gone. . . . Now I will make your name great, like the names of the greatest men on earth."* —2 Samuel 7:9

23

1 & 2 KINGS

THE LIMITS OF HUMAN RULE

WRITTEN c. 561–539 BC by an unknown author

PURPOSE To demonstrate the value of obeying God and the danger of disobeying.

SUMMARY

Originally one book with 2 Kings, 1 Kings covers King Solomon's impressive achievements: wise governing, completion of the temple in Jerusalem, and expansion of the kingdom. The book also explains his eventual downfall: marrying many foreign wives and worshiping their gods. After Solomon's death, civil war tears the kingdom apart.

The book of 2 Kings records the history of the kings of the Northern Kingdom (Israel) and the Southern Kingdom (Judah). Despite occasional spiritual reforms—such as King Hezekiah's and King Josiah's reforms—the sins of Israel and Judah eventually result in their kingdoms being conquered and their people exiled by the Assyrian and Babylonian Empires.

OUTLINE

1 Kings
- King Solomon's reign (1–10)
- The kingdom splits (11–16)
- Elijah's ministry (17–22)

2 Kings
- Elisha's ministry (1–8)
- Kings of Israel and Judah (9–16)
- Fall of Israel (17)
- Hezekiah, Josiah; fall of Judah (18–25)

JESUS IN KINGS God's promise to David of a continuous descendant on the throne of Israel is the historical and theological basis for the coming of a Messiah, one who would unify God's people, redeem them, and reconcile them with God. This promise was fulfilled in Jesus, the Messiah, who saves Israel and the world.

KEY VERSES

Solomon asks God: *"Give your servant a discerning heart to govern your people and to distinguish between right and wrong."*
—1 Kings 3:9

King Hezekiah's prayer: *"LORD, the God of Israel . . . you alone are God over all the kingdoms of the earth."*
—2 Kings 19:15

Although in our English Bibles there are two books of Kings, the Hebrew text has only one book. The reason to divide it was purely practical. When the book was translated into Greek—the Septuagint—the translated text was significantly longer. To make the book fit better in the scrolls, the translators decided to break Samuel and Kings. Originally, Samuel was called 1 and 2 books of Kings, and Kings was divided into 3 and 4 books of Kings.

1 & 2 CHRONICLES

STILL THE PEOPLE OF GOD

WRITTEN c. 450–400 BC by an unknown author
(possibly Ezra)

PURPOSE To encourage the exiles who returned to Judah.

SUMMARY
First Chronicles is a history (or chronicle) of King David's reign.
Both 1 and 2 Chronicles were written for the Jews returning
from exile, many centuries after David, to encourage them by
connecting them to their past. Their promise and hope for a
restored Israel could be found in remembering what God did
in their history.

Second Chronicles covers history from King Solomon all the
way through the fall of Judah and the decree allowing the exiles
to return home. This history is meant to inspire the people to
remain faithful to God as he has been to them, and also to warn
them about the consequences of complacency, rebellion,
and idolatry.

OUTLINE

1 Chronicles
- Genealogies (1–9)
- David's victories (10–20)
- David's census (21–27)
- David's final days (28–29)

2 Chronicles
- King Solomon (1–9)
- Kings of Judah (10–35)
- Fall of Judah, exile, and the decree to return to Judah (36)

JESUS IN CHRONICLES

In Chronicles, God began to fulfill his promise to restore Israel by bringing them back from exile. The hopeful ending anticipates a time that goes back to David's kingdom, with Israel once again a united people in the Promised Land. In Jesus, God showed his intention to restore humanity as a whole through David's descendant, the Messiah, God's own Son. Jesus is the fulfillment of that ancient promise to save humanity from the bondage of sin, restore them to a relationship with God, and renew their hearts and minds.

As with Samuel and Kings, Chronicles was originally one book. When the Jewish translators made the Greek translation of the Hebrew Bible—the Septuagint—the book was too long to fit into one scroll. For practical reasons, they divided the book into 1 and 2 Chronicles.

KEY VERSES

God's promise to David: *"I will set [your son] over my house and my kingdom forever."*
—1 Chronicles 17:14

"As for us, the LORD is our God, and we have not forsaken him."
—2 Chronicles 13:10

EZRA

HISTORY OF THE FIRST AND SECOND WAVES OF JEWS WHO RETURNED TO JERUSALEM

WRITTEN c. 400s BC by Ezra

PURPOSE To provide an account of the exiles' return and restoration.

SUMMARY The book of Ezra shows how God is faithful to his promise to restore his people. After they spend decades in exile in Babylon and Persia, King Cyrus of Persia allows the Jews to return to their homeland. The first wave of returning Jews is led by Zerubbabel, who oversees the rebuilding of the temple in Jerusalem. The second wave is led by Ezra, a court scribe and priest, who guides the community in spiritual renewal.

OUTLINE
- First return led by Zerubbabel (1–2)
- The temple is rebuilt (3–6)
- Second return led by Ezra (7–8)
- Spiritual restoration (9–10)

JESUS IN EZRA The book of Ezra shows the fulfillment of God's promises to restore Israel. However, the promise was only partially fulfilled. The complete fulfillment of God's promise occurs in Jesus.

KEY VERSE
"[The Lord] is good; his love toward Israel endures forever."
—Ezra 3:11

NEHEMIAH

HISTORY OF THE THIRD WAVE OF JEWS WHO RETURNED TO JERUSALEM

WRITTEN   c. 400s BC by Ezra

PURPOSE   To provide an account of the exiles' return and restoration.

SUMMARY   Originally one book with Ezra, the book of Nehemiah continues where Ezra left off. Nehemiah is a cupbearer to a Persian king who allows him to lead a group of Jews to Jerusalem to rebuild the crumbling walls of the city. This enormous task is completed in only 52 days despite much opposition. Whereas Ezra led a spiritual restoration, Nehemiah leads a political and physical restoration of Jerusalem and its inhabitants.

OUTLINE
- Third return led by Nehemiah (1–2)
- Rebuilding the walls (3)
- Threats and persecution (4–7)
- Renewal and dedication (8–13)

JESUS IN NEHEMIAH   The book of Nehemiah shows the fulfillment of God's promises to restore Israel. However, the promise was only partially fulfilled. The complete fulfillment of God's promise occurs in Jesus.

KEY VERSE
"Do not grieve, for the joy of the LORD is your strength."
—Nehemiah 8:10

ESTHER

A STORY OF COURAGE IN DANGEROUS TIMES

WRITTEN   c. 400s BC by an unknown author

PURPOSE   To demonstrate that God is in control in all circumstances.

SUMMARY   The book of Esther is the story of a young Jewish woman thrown into a world of political intrigue and power plays in the Persian court in Susa. The story takes place while the Jews were in exile. Esther becomes queen to Persian King Xerxes I (Ahasuerus). She makes courageous choices to save her people from being slaughtered by their enemies.

OUTLINE
- Esther becomes queen (1–2)
- Haman's plot against the Jews (3)
- Esther's plan to protect her people (4–6)
- Haman's downfall (7)
- The Jews are saved and Purim is established (8–10)

JESUS IN ESTHER   Although God is not explicitly named in the book, his presence is unmistakable throughout the story. In our busy lives, we often go on living as if Jesus were not present. Yet, as in Esther, he is ever present and interested in our lives.

KEY VERSE
Mordecai said to Queen Esther: *"And who knows but that you have come to your royal position for such a time as this?"*
—Esther 4:14

Poetry & Wisdom Books

What Are the Poetry and Wisdom Books?

This section is composed of five books, four of which are written in poetry: Job (most of it), Psalms, Proverbs, and Song of Songs. Ecclesiastes is written mostly in prose.

Poetry has a unique ability to express deep feelings and thoughts in affective and beautiful ways. For that reason, poetry is the perfect instrument for wisdom.

The Poetry and Wisdom Books:

- Do not deal directly with Israel's life at a specific time in history.
- Reflect on the life of God's people and their relationship with God in a more general way.
- Deal with questions about human suffering, death, and what makes a good life.

Poetry and Wisdom Books Today

These books continue to be important for Christians today. Their main themes shape the hearts and minds of God's people:

- Praise and prayer
- Guidance for holy lives
- Our inner relationship with God and our relationships with others around us

JOB

A STORY OF SUFFERING AND TRUST

WRITTEN Date and author are unknown

PURPOSE To show the sovereignty of God and to illustrate faithfulness in the midst of suffering.

SUMMARY Though the story of Job is set in an unknown place called Uz probably around the time of Abraham, its themes of human suffering and God's wisdom are timeless. In the story, Job is a "blameless and upright" (1:1) man who finds his life overturned. Despite his intense pain, Job does "not sin by charging God with wrongdoing" (1:22). In the end, Job is reminded that God is sovereign over all creation.

OUTLINE
- Prose: Job tested by losing everything (1–2)
- Poetry: Dialogues (3–41)
  - Job and his friends: Eliphaz, Bildad, Zophar (3–31)
  - Elihu's speech (32–37)
  - God's answer to Job (38–41)
- Prose: Job restored (42)

JESUS IN JOB Jesus experienced suffering and can empathize with our own suffering (Hebrews 4:15). Trusting in Jesus does not give us all the answers to our doubts and questions, but it does give peace and comfort in times of suffering.

KEY VERSE

"I know that my redeemer lives, and that in the end he will stand on the earth. And after my skin has been destroyed, yet in my flesh I will see God."—Job 19:25–26

PSALMS

A COLLECTION OF POETIC SONGS

WRITTEN c. 1000–450 BC by David (73 psalms), Asaph (12 psalms), the sons of Korah (11 psalms), and others

PURPOSE To communicate with God and worship him.

SUMMARY The book of Psalms is a collection of songs (psalms) written and compiled over a long time span. It can be separated into five collections (books).

OUTLINE

BOOK	PSALMS	THEMES
1	1–41	Prayers of lament and expressions of confidence in God's salvation.
2	42–72	Community laments. The book ends with a royal psalm.
3	73–89	Prayers of lament and distress more intense and bleak than in books 1 and 2.
4	90–106	The Lord reigns! Book 4 presents the answers to the bleakness of book 3.
5	107–150	God is in control, faithful, and good. He will redeem his people.

JESUS IN PSALMS When Jesus said that all of the Scriptures spoke of him he specifically mentioned the psalms (Luke 24:44). The New Testament writers quote many of the psalm texts in connection to Jesus being the promised Messiah.

KEY VERSE *"My mouth will speak in praise of the Lord. Let every creature praise his holy name for ever and ever."* —Psalms 145:21

PROVERBS

WISDOM FOR GODLY LIVING

WRITTEN   c. 900s–700s BC by King Solomon and others

PURPOSE   To gain wisdom and instruction for prudent behavior and doing what is right (1:1–3).

SUMMARY   The book of Proverbs invites readers to make life-changing decisions between wisdom and foolishness. The readers "hear" from both Lady Wisdom and Lady Folly (Foolishness). Their invitations become alternatives between a path of wisdom that leads to life and a path of foolishness that leads to death.

OUTLINE
- Invitations to choose wisdom or foolishness (1–9)
- Proverbs of Solomon (10–21)
- Thirty sayings and other wise words (22–24)
- Solomon's sayings (25–29)
- Words of Agur and Lemuel (30:1–31:9)
- Poem of the wise woman (31:10–31)

JESUS IN PROVERBS   Jesus embodies God's wisdom (1 Corinthians 1:30). In him "are hidden all the treasures of wisdom and knowledge" (Colossians 2:3).

KEY VERSE
"Trust in the LORD with all your heart and lean not on your own understanding; in all your ways submit to him, and he will make your paths straight." —Proverbs 3:5–6

ECCLESIASTES

SEARCHING FOR MEANING AND TRUTH

WRITTEN   c. 971–931 BC by King Solomon or possibly by different authors in the 500s BC

PURPOSE   To examine what a meaningful life is.

SUMMARY   The author of Ecclesiastes wants to make sense out of life, wisdom, and truth. At first, he proposes that everything is meaningless (vanity). After careful observation, the pursuit of all worldly pleasures, an assessment of wisdom, and an analysis of the purpose of life, he concludes that a meaningful life is not found in those frivolous pursuits. Instead, it is found in pursuing God as our number one priority, remembering and obeying our Creator.

OUTLINE
- Everything is meaningless (1–2)
- A time for everything (3–5)
- Life is not always fair (6–10)
- Remember and obey God (11–12)

JESUS IN ECCLESIASTES   The end of the search for truth and meaning is Jesus Christ. Only by seeking Christ and believing in his death and resurrection will we find righteousness, salvation, and true meaning.

KEY VERSE
"Fear God and keep his commandments, for this is the duty of all mankind." —Ecclesiastes 12:13

SONG OF SONGS

A LOVE SONG

WRITTEN   c. 971–931 BC by King Solomon and possibly others as late as the 500s BC

PURPOSE   To illustrate the joy of authentic love found in marriage.

SUMMARY   Song of Songs is a collection of love poems declaring mutual love and affection between the lover and his beloved. The poems are written to present us with the way things should be within a loving, covenant relationship.

OUTLINE
- Courtship (1–2)
- Wedding (3–4)
- Loving relationship (5–8)

JESUS IN SONG OF SONGS   The apostle Paul wrote, "Husbands, love your wives, just as Christ loved the church and gave himself up for her" (Ephesians 5:25). The church is the bride of Christ. As Christ's bride, we are his beloved and participate in a loving, passionate, and intimate relationship with him. Although Song of Songs is not primarily an allegory of our relationship with Jesus, it is a superb example of a loving relationship with our Lord and Savior.

KEY VERSE
"I am my beloved's and my beloved is mine."—Song of Songs 6:3

PROPHETIC BOOKS

What Are the Prophetic Books?

The Prophetic Books record the ministries of the prophets whom God sent to encourage, warn, and guide his people. These books are divided into two sections:

- The Major Prophets: Isaiah through Daniel
- The Minor Prophets: Hosea through Malachi (the last book of the Old Testament)

These books are called *major* and *minor* because of their length—from very long (sixty-six chapters in Isaiah) to very short (only one chapter in Obadiah).

What Is Prophecy?

Biblical prophets were God's servants especially called to be his witnesses. In the Old Testament, prophecy was a tool that God used to communicate his will to his people. God sent prophets to his people during times of crisis, such as:

- Military threats against God's people.
- When the people rebelled against God's will.
- When hope seemed all but lost.
- When the people needed comfort in difficult times.

Old Testament prophets brought the word of God to the people, and they interceded on behalf of the people before God. As Scripture says, "Surely the Sovereign Lord does nothing without revealing his plan to his servants the prophets" (Amos 3:7).

The Prophetic Books

NAME	APPROX. DATE BC	AUDIENCE
ISAIAH	735–681	Judah
JEREMIAH	626–582	Judah
LAMENTATIONS	586	Judah
EZEKIEL	593–571	Exiles in Babylon
DANIEL	605–535	Exiles in Babylon and Persia
HOSEA	752–722	Northern Kingdom of Israel
JOEL	500s–400s	Judah and surrounding nations
AMOS	760–753	Northern Kingdom of Israel
OBADIAH	586	Edom and the people of Judah
JONAH	783–753	Nineveh (capital of the Assyrian Empire)
MICAH	738–698	Samaria and Jerusalem
NAHUM	663–612	Nineveh (capital of the Assyrian Empire)
HABAKKUK	609–598	All God's people
ZEPHANIAH	641–628	Judah and surrounding nations
HAGGAI	520	Judah and Jerusalem
ZECHARIAH	520–518	Judah and Jerusalem
MALACHI	400s	Jerusalem

SUBJECT
God's judgment and salvation
God's judgment, wrath, and destruction of Jerusalem
A lament for the destruction of Jerusalem
God's presence with his people in exile
God's sovereignty and future redemption
Israel's unfaithfulness to their covenant with God
The great and dreadful day of the Lord
God's judgment upon Israel for their injustice and lack of mercy
God's judgment upon Edom
God's judgment upon Nineveh; yet God's mercy extends to all
God's judgment upon Israel and Judah for their wickedness
God's judgment upon Nineveh for their cruelty against God's people
God's judgment, justice, love, and mercy
A call to repentance before the coming judgment on the day of the Lord
A call to rebuild the temple and a message of hope
A call to rebuild the temple and a message of future glory
A call to spiritual renewal

ISAIAH

JUDGMENT AND SALVATION

WRITTEN c. 735–681 BC by the prophet Isaiah

PURPOSE To convince the people that salvation is possible through repentance for sin and hope in the coming Messiah.

SUMMARY With powerful enemies on all sides and war looming, God's people formed political and military alliances with pagan nations in hopes of protecting themselves. God commissions the prophet Isaiah to bring messages of impending judgment if God's people continue to look for their salvation in the strength and gods of other nations.

OUTLINE
- Condemnation (1–39)
- Comfort in exile (40–55)
- Future hope (56–66)

JESUS IN ISAIAH Jesus is the promised Messiah, a descendant of King David (Isaiah 11:1–2). In his death and resurrection, Jesus inaugurated a new kingdom—God's kingdom. When Jesus returns, there will be a new heaven and a new earth (Isaiah 65:17–19).

KEY VERSE
"For to us a child is born, to us a son is given, and the government will be on his shoulders. And he will be called Wonderful Counselor, Mighty God, Everlasting Father, Prince of Peace." —Isaiah 9:6

JEREMIAH
JUDGMENT, WRATH, AND WEEPING

WRITTEN   c. 626–582 BC by the prophet Jeremiah

PURPOSE   To warn the people of destruction and to remind them of their sin in hopes of bringing them to repentance.

SUMMARY   Jeremiah brings a message of judgment against the people of Judah. He hopes that heartfelt repentance by God's people will deter God's wrath.

OUTLINE
- Jeremiah's call and message of judgment (1–10)
- Warnings of disaster and exile (11–28)
- New covenant and restoration (29–39)
- Fall of Jerusalem (40–52)

JESUS IN JEREMIAH   In Jeremiah, the Messiah is foretold as a righteous Branch from the line of David. At the Passover meal on the night Jesus was betrayed, he took the cup and referenced Jeremiah 31:31, saying, "This cup is the new covenant in my blood, which is poured out for you" (Luke 22:20). Jesus' death and resurrection instituted the new covenant Jeremiah prophesied.

KEY VERSE
*"For I know the plans I have for you," declares the L*ORD, *"plans to prosper you and not to harm you, plans to give you hope and a future."* —Jeremiah 29:11

LAMENTATIONS
DIRGE POEM (LAMENT)

WRITTEN c. 586 BC by the prophet Jeremiah

PURPOSE To express the despair of the people of Judah over the loss of their land, city, and temple.

SUMMARY Lamentations is an eyewitness account of the destruction of Jerusalem. The grief expressed in these poems reveals deep regret and desire for the restoration of God's people.

OUTLINE
- Sorrow of captives (1)
- Anger with Jerusalem (2)
- Hope and mercy (3)
- Punishment (4)
- Restoration (5)

JESUS IN LAMENTATIONS So where is Christ to be found in this book? In the pain and the suffering itself. The language of verses 2:15–16 and 3:15—"he has filled me with bitter herbs and given me gall to drink"—appears at the cross—"There they offered Jesus wine to drink, mixed with gall" (Matthew 27:34). God knows our suffering! The language of Lamentations expresses Christ's anguish and sorrow over sin and its terrible price.

KEY VERSE
"His compassions never fail. They are new every morning; great is your faithfulness."—Lamentations 3:22–23

EZEKIEL

PROPHECIES AND VISIONS OF GOD'S PRESENCE

WRITTEN   c. 593–571 BC by the prophet Ezekiel

PURPOSE   To call God's people in exile to be faithful to God, who is still among them.

SUMMARY   The book of Ezekiel asks a crucial question: Is God present with us or has he abandoned us? Through prophecies and visions, Ezekiel communicates God's message that if the exiles were to walk humbly with God, then God's presence with them would be a source of peace, life, and future restoration.

OUTLINE
- Call of Ezekiel (1–3)
- Coming captivity of Judah (4–24)
- Judgment of other nations (25–32)
- Restoration of God's people (33–48)

JESUS IN EZEKIEL   Some of the most important imagery that Jesus used to explain his ministry to his disciples comes from the book of Ezekiel: Jesus is the true temple, the Shepherd King (Ezekiel 34), and the source of living waters (Ezekiel 47:1–2; John 4:10–14; 7:38–39).

KEY VERSE
"I will give you a new heart and put a new spirit in you; I will remove from your heart of stone and give you a heart of flesh."
—Ezekiel 36:26

DANIEL

LIFE IN EXILE AND VISIONS OF THE FUTURE

WRITTEN c. 605–535 BC by the prophet Daniel

PURPOSE To convince the exiles that God is sovereign and to provide them with a vision of their future redemption.

SUMMARY The first part of the book tells about Daniel and his friends in the Babylonian court. This account shows God's people how to obey God while in the midst of a foreign, hostile land. The second part of the book includes Daniel's visions. The purpose of these visions is to reassure God's people that God is in control.

OUTLINE
- Daniel and his friends (1–6)
- Daniel's visions (7–12)

JESUS IN DANIEL The phrase "son of man" is just the Hebrew way of saying human being (8:17). But the name takes on a special significance in Daniel 7:13–14, where it describes someone who rides on the clouds, is given an everlasting kingdom, and is worshiped. The term became a title that referred to the coming Messiah. It was the title Jesus most preferred when speaking of himself.

KEY VERSE
"In the time of those kings, the God of heaven will set up a kingdom that will never be destroyed, nor will it be left to another people. It will crush all those kingdoms and bring them to an end, but it will itself endure forever." —Daniel 2:44

HOSEA

WARNINGS TO A SPIRITUALLY ADULTEROUS NATION

WRITTEN c. 752–722 BC by the prophet Hosea

PURPOSE To illustrate Israel's spiritual adultery and warn of destruction.

SUMMARY Hosea is a prophet during the decline and fall of the Northern Kingdom of Israel. God commands him to marry an adulterous woman as a real-life illustration of God's never-failing love for the people of Israel, who were being unfaithful to their covenant relationship with God.

OUTLINE
- Hosea and his unfaithful wife (1–3)
- Unfaithful Israel (4–10)
- God's love and anger (11–13)
- Israel's hope (14)

JESUS IN HOSEA Jesus fulfilled Hosea's prophecy by redeeming a people who broke God's heart through unfaithfulness. Jesus delivered God's people from the slavery of sin and death, often equated to the bondage the Israelites experienced in Egypt. Jesus, the Lion of Judah, roars upon his victory over the grave that delivers us from our Egypts and Assyrias, from all those places in our lives that hold us captive.

KEY VERSE
"I desire mercy, not sacrifice, and acknowledgment of God rather than burnt offerings." —Hosea 6:6

JOEL

PROPHECIES ABOUT THE GREAT AND DREADFUL DAY OF THE LORD

WRITTEN   Possibly c. 500s–400s BC by the prophet Joel

PURPOSE   To call Judah to repentance in order to avoid judgment.

SUMMARY   Joel warns God's people about the judgment they will face on the day of the Lord, but also of the amazing blessings God will pour out on those who heed the word of the Lord.

OUTLINE
- Locust plague (1:1–20)
- Army from the north (2:1–27)
- Day of the Lord (2:28–3:21)

JESUS IN JOEL   The prophet Joel anticipated the day of the Lord as a great and dreadful day. It was a day of salvation and judgment. Jesus came to the world to save it (John 3:16), and one day will come to judge it (Acts 10:42; 17:31). The prophet visualized a single day to come. Yet, Jesus is fulfilling the prophecy in two parts: in his first coming about 2,000 years ago and when he returns in power, glory, and victory.

KEY VERSE
"I will pour out my Spirit on all people. Your sons and daughters will prophesy, your old men will dream dreams, your young men will see visions."—Joel 2:28 (See Acts 2:14–21)

AMOS

WARNINGS TO A SOCIETY GONE AWRY

WRITTEN c. 760–753 BC by the prophet Amos

PURPOSE To accuse and judge Israel for injustice and lack of mercy.

SUMMARY Amos prophesies during a time of great material prosperity and peace. The people have become apathetic toward God, corrupting their worship and treating the poor unjustly. Amos, a shepherd from a small village, is sent by God to tell the people to change their ways or else face the judgment of God.

OUTLINE
- Israel and its neighbors (1–4)
- Call to repentance (5:1–17)
- False religion, injustice, pride (5:18–6:14)
- Judgment and restoration (7–9)

JESUS IN AMOS Jesus echoes Amos continuously. He commanded his followers to feed the hungry, to clothe the naked, to welcome the outcasts, to care for the sick, and to visit the imprisoned (Matthew 25:31–46). Jesus also criticized the religious leaders for offering "lip service" to God, but not truly living a God-pleasing life (Matthew 15:1–20).

KEY VERSE
"Seek good, not evil, that you may live. Then the Lord God Almighty will be with you." —Amos 5:14

OBADIAH

A VISION AGAINST EDOM

WRITTEN   c. 586 BC by the prophet Obadiah

PURPOSE   To prophesy against Edom.

SUMMARY   Obadiah, the shortest book in the Old Testament, judges the people of Edom for their disregard and mistreatment of the Israelites in Judah. Edom was a small kingdom southwest of the Dead Sea with a long history of hostility with Israel. In time, the Babylonian empire destroyed Edom.

OUTLINE (verses)
- Judgment of Edom (1–9)
- Edom's violations (10–14)
- Israel's victory (15–21)

JESUS IN OBADIAH   Obadiah promised the people of Judah that God will keep the promise he made to Abraham. His people will receive redemption and their promised inheritance. Jesus fulfilled the promises made to Abraham. Those who believe in Jesus receive redemption and their promised inheritance (Colossians 1:9–14; Hebrews 9:15).

KEY VERSE
"Because of the violence against your brother Jacob [the Israelites], you will be covered with shame; you will be destroyed forever."
—Obadiah 10

JONAH

A STORY OF GOD'S MERCY

WRITTEN   c. 783–753 BC by the prophet Jonah

PURPOSE   To show that God loves all people.

SUMMARY   It takes a storm, a great fish, and God's relentless pursuit of Jonah to get him to obey God's call to prophesy in the wicked and dangerous city of Nineveh. When Jonah does go to Nineveh, the Ninevites repent and God spares them from wrath. God's mercy extends to all people, even those who appear beyond redemption.

OUTLINE
- Jonah flees from God (1)
- Jonah prays inside the great fish (2)
- Jonah prophesies in Nineveh (3)
- Jonah resents God's mercy (4)

JESUS IN JONAH   Jesus compared himself to Jonah (Matthew 12:40–41). First, Jonah spent three days in the belly of a great fish and Jesus spent three days in the belly of the earth. Second, Jonah preached repentance to the Gentiles in Nineveh and God showed them mercy. In the same way, the gospel of Christ will be preached to the Gentiles and they too will receive the grace and mercy of God.

KEY VERSE
"You are a gracious and compassionate God, slow to anger and abounding in love."—Jonah 4:2

MICAH

A CALL TO SEEK JUSTICE, LOVE MERCY, AND WALK HUMBLY

WRITTEN   c. 738–698 BC by the prophet Micah

PURPOSE   To warn people of God's judgment and to offer hope.

SUMMARY   Micah prophesies against the leaders of his people for their injustice, greed, and pride. Micah brings word of the destruction of Samaria and Jerusalem, but also proclaims a vision of future redemption and forgiveness.

OUTLINE
- Judgment and deliverance (1–5)
- Confession and restoration (6–7)

JESUS IN MICAH   Micah predicts the birthplace of Jesus in Bethlehem, but more than that, this prophecy states that this "shepherd" will lead God's people into an eternal kingdom that will reach to the ends of the earth (Micah 5:2–4). When the angel Gabriel announced the birth of Jesus to Mary, he told her that Jesus "will reign over Jacob's descendants forever; his kingdom will never end" (Luke 1:33).

KEY VERSE
"What does the LORD require of you? To act justly and to love mercy and to walk humbly with your God." —Micah 6:8

NAHUM

PROPHECY ABOUT THE DESTRUCTION OF NINEVEH

WRITTEN   c. 663–612 BC by the prophet Nahum

PURPOSE   To pronounce judgment on Nineveh.

SUMMARY   God calls Nahum to warn about judgment against the Assyrian capital of Nineveh for their cruelty and idolatry. Though God is slow to anger, he will avenge his people for the atrocities Assyria committed against them. In 612 BC, Nahum's prophecy was fulfilled when Assyria fell to the Babylonian Empire.

OUTLINE
- Mercy and justice (1)
- Nineveh will fall (2)
- Woe to Nineveh (3)

JESUS IN NAHUM   God is a stern judge, but he is also merciful. God's mercy reached its culmination with Jesus on the cross. The apostle Paul writes, "For God did not appoint us to suffer wrath but to receive salvation through our Lord Jesus Christ. He died for us so that, whether we are awake or asleep, we may live together with him" (1 Thessalonians 5:9–10).

KEY VERSE
"The LORD is slow to anger but great in power; the LORD will not leave the guilty unpunished." —Nahum 1:3

HABAKKUK

A PROPHET ASKS GOD ABOUT JUSTICE AND MERCY

WRITTEN c. 609–598 BC by the prophet Habakkuk

PURPOSE To affirm that the wicked will not prevail in the end.

SUMMARY Habakkuk asks the question: Why does God let people get away with evil? Habakkuk grapples with how God's anger and justice relate to his love and mercy. At the end of the book, Habakkuk recognizes that no matter what doubts he has, he knows that God will always render a righteous judgment in the end.

OUTLINE
- First complaint and answer (1:1–11)
- Second complaint and answer (1:12–2:20)
- Prayer of praise (3:1–19)

JESUS IN HABAKKUK Habakkuk recognized that God would eventually bring justice and redeem his people (Habakkuk 3:13). God's ultimate redemption comes to completion in Jesus Christ. By the grace of God, Jesus crushed wickedness. On the cross, Jesus overcame sin, death, and Satan, offering the world God's love, mercy, and justice (Ephesians 2:1–10).

KEY VERSE
"I will rejoice in the LORD, I will be joyful in God my Savior."
—Habakkuk 3:18

ZEPHANIAH

WARNINGS ABOUT JUDGMENT ON THE DAY OF THE LORD

WRITTEN   c. 641–628 BC by the prophet Zephaniah

PURPOSE   To motivate Judah to repentance.

SUMMARY   Zephaniah prophesies during the reign of King Josiah, the last of Judah's good kings, who instituted spiritual reforms among the people. Zephaniah proclaims that the doom of the day of the Lord will be devastating to Judah and their neighbors unless they repent. He urges them to act quickly!

OUTLINE
- The day of the Lord (1)
- Judgment on Judah and other nations (2)
- A remnant restored (3)

JESUS IN ZEPHANIAH   The day of the Lord is inevitable and on that day, God will judge the nations and make new heavens and a new earth. All who confess Jesus as their Redeemer will be saved (2 Peter 3:10–13).

KEY VERSE
"The great day of the LORD is near—near and coming quickly."
—Zephaniah 1:14

HAGGAI

A MESSAGE TO REBUILD THE TEMPLE

WRITTEN c. 520 BC by the prophet Haggai

PURPOSE To urge the people to complete rebuilding the temple.

SUMMARY In Haggai's time, the Jews had returned to Jerusalem after 70 years of exile. At first they enthusiastically began rebuilding the temple, but soon fell into apathy. God's message through Haggai challenges the people to complete the task at hand because God is with them. The temple was completed four years later in 516 BC.

OUTLINE
- Rebuild the temple (1)
- Be strong, be holy, be blessed (2)

JESUS IN HAGGAI The temple and Zerubbabel foreshadowed the future ministry of the coming Messiah.
The Messiah would be the desire of all nations (Haggai 2:6–7), chosen, authoritative, like a signet ring on God's hand. God would once more shake the world and fill his temple with the glory of Christ.

KEY VERSE
"Is it a time for you yourselves to be living in your paneled houses, while [the Lord's] house remains a ruin? Give careful thought to your ways." —Haggai 1:4–5

ZECHARIAH

VISIONS AND MESSAGES ABOUT THE LORD'S REIGN OVER ALL

WRITTEN   c. 520–518 BC by the prophet Zechariah

PURPOSE   To give hope to the remnant in Israel.

SUMMARY   Zechariah, a prophet of priestly lineage, traveled to Jerusalem from exile with the group who returned under Zerubbabel. Along with the prophet Haggai, Zechariah encourages the people to rebuild the temple. Zechariah's visions and messages of hope look forward to a time when God's reign will be recognized throughout the world.

OUTLINE
- Visions and messages (1–8)
- Oracles against the nations (9–14)

JESUS IN ZECHARIAH   The "Servant Branch" in Zechariah 3:8 and 6:11–13 is a Messianic figure who will save his people. In Zechariah 6:9–15, the Branch is described as both a priest and a king. Jesus fulfilled God's promises of the Branch by being a servant of God and our ultimate High Priest and King.

KEY VERSE
"'Not by might nor by power, but by my Spirit,' says the LORD Almighty."—Zechariah 4:6

MALACHI

THE COMING DAY OF THE LORD

WRITTEN   c. 400s BC by the prophet Malachi

PURPOSE   To examine Judah's actions and make sure God has priority.

SUMMARY   Malachi calls for spiritual renewal among a people who had largely given up on God. The people had returned from exile and completed rebuilding the temple, but the blessings that Haggai and Zechariah prophesied about had yet to materialize. The people began to doubt God's blessings. With six prophetic speeches, Malachi urges the people to recognize their own unfaithfulness—shorting tithes, bringing unacceptable sacrifices, ignoring God's law—because the day of reckoning, the day of the Lord, is coming.

OUTLINE
- Six prophetic speeches (1–3)
- The day of the Lord (4)

JESUS IN MALACHI   In Malachi, God promised to send his messenger. In fact, God would show up in the temple. God appeared in his temple in Christ (John 2:13–22). God's way was prepared by John the Baptist, who came in the spirit of Elijah (Malachi 4:5; Matthew 17:11–13; Luke 1:13–17). Jesus' purpose was not merely to judge but to save.

KEY VERSE
"Bring the whole tithe into the storehouse, that there may be food in my house. Test me in this," says the LORD Almighty, "and see if I will not throw open the floodgates of heaven and pour out so much blessing that there will not be room enough to store it."
 —Malachi 3:10

THE NEW TESTAMENT

Books of the New Testament

The New Testament consists of twenty-seven books. The four Gospels narrate the life of Jesus Christ and Acts tells the story of the first Christians. The twenty-one epistles are letters from early church leaders to churches and believers. The book of Revelation is the only book that is written in an apocalyptic style; in other words, the book relates its message through signs, symbols, dreams, and visions.

GOSPELS & ACTS	EPISTLES & REVELATION	
Matthew	*Paul's Epistles:*	*General Epistles:*
Mark	Romans	Hebrews
Luke	1 Corinthians	James
John	2 Corinthians	1 Peter
	Galatians	2 Peter
Acts	Ephesians	1 John
	Philippians	2 John
	Colossians	3 John
	1 Thessalonians	Jude
	2 Thessalonians	
	1 Timothy	Revelation
	2 Timothy	
	Titus	
	Philemon	

Holy Land: New Testament

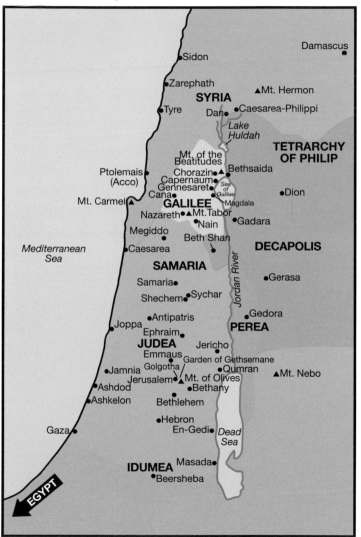

Damascus

Sidon

Zarephath

SYRIA
Mt. Hermon

Tyre
Dan
Caesarea-Philippi

Lake
Huldah

TETRARCHY
OF PHILIP

Mt. of the
Beatitudes
Chorazin
Bethsaida

Ptolemais
(Acco)
Capernaum
Gennesaret
Sea
of
Galilee
Dion

Mt. Carmel
Cana
Magdala

GALILEE

Nazareth
Mt. Tabor
Nain
Gadara

Megiddo
Beth Shan

DECAPOLIS

Mediterranean
Sea
Caesarea

SAMARIA

Samaria
Jordan River
Gerasa

Shechem
Sychar

Antipatris
Gedora

Joppa
PEREA

Ephraim

JUDEA
Jericho

Emmaus
Garden of Gethsemane

Jamnia
Golgotha
Qumran
Mt. Nebo

Ashdod
Jerusalem
Mt. of Olives

Ashkelon
Bethany

Bethlehem

Hebron

Gaza
En-Gedi
Dead
Sea

IDUMEA
Masada

Beersheba

EGYPT

GOSPELS

What Are the Gospels?

The word *gospel* comes from the Greek word *euangelion*, which means "good news." The Gospels tell the good news about the actions and teachings of Jesus. God's promises to his people in the Old Testament are now fulfilled in Jesus. We do not find just one story about Jesus. Rather, we find four: Matthew, Mark, Luke, and John.

The Synoptic Gospels and John

The word *synoptic* means "seen together." It refers to the first three Gospels: Matthew, Mark, and Luke. These Gospels often contain related stories in very similar language. The Gospel of John, however, includes material that the other writers do not, and the wording is often different.

GOSPEL	AUDIENCE	FOCUS
MATTHEW	A Jewish cultural world	Jesus as Messiah
MARK	A Greek cultural world	Jesus as the Son of Man
LUKE	A Gentile world	Jesus as the Savior of the world
JOHN	The whole world	Jesus as the Son of God

MATTHEW

JESUS, THE PROMISED MESSIAH

WRITTEN   c. AD 60 by Matthew (Levi), a tax collector and one of Jesus' twelve disciples, to a Jewish Christian audience

PURPOSE   To show Jesus as the Son of David, the kingly Messiah who fulfills prophecy.

SUMMARY   Matthew focuses on the many ways Jesus fulfilled Old Testament prophecies and God's grand plan of salvation for Israel and the world. Most Jews at the time of Jesus expected the Messiah to be a military leader who would liberate them from the Romans. But Jesus was an unexpected Messiah. He did liberate people, but not from Rome; rather, he freed them from sin and death.

> The word *Messiah* is derived from a Hebrew word meaning "anointed one," like the Greek word *Christ*. The term referred to one who would come to rule Israel, restore the kingdom of David, and bring peace and prosperity to God's people.

OUTLINE

- Preparing the way (1–4)
- Jesus in Galilee (5–18)
- Jesus' last days in Judea and Jerusalem (19–27)
- Resurrection and Great Commission (28)

KEY VERSE

"Go and make disciples of all nations, baptizing them in the name of the Father and of the Son and of the Holy Spirit."
—Matthew 28:19 (The Great Commission)

MARK

JESUS, THE SUFFERING SON OF MAN

WRITTEN c. AD 50s by John Mark, a disciple of Peter and a friend of Paul, to a Gentile (possibly Roman) Christian audience

PURPOSE To show Jesus as the suffering Son of Man sent to serve and not be served.

SUMMARY Mark shows that the good news of God's rule over all things is revealed by Jesus' teachings and miracles. Jesus, the Son of Man, is God's active agent, his power in the world, and his means of defeating sin, death, and the devil. Yet Jesus, our kingly champion, appears in humility. Jesus shares in the suffering that probably many of Mark's original audience experienced in persecution for their faith.

> The phrase *Son of Man* expresses the promise of a king, one who would defeat the forces of evil and establish God's eternal kingdom.

OUTLINE
- Beginning of Jesus' ministry (1)
- Jesus' public ministry (2–10)
- In Jerusalem (11–16)

KEY VERSE
"For even the Son of Man did not come to be served, but to serve, and to give his life as a ransom for many." —Mark 10:45

LUKE

JESUS, THE SAVIOR OF THE WORLD

WRITTEN   c. AD 60–62 by Luke (also the author of Acts), likely a doctor and Gentile fellow traveler with Paul, to a Gentile audience

PURPOSE   To show Jesus as the Savior of the world who has compassion for all people.

SUMMARY   Luke emphasizes how the good news of Jesus is for everyone. He also focuses on the presence and power of the Holy Spirit (4:14); the fact that God's kingdom is here and belongs to his children (12:32); Jesus' care and help for the poor and disadvantaged (6:17–19); and the importance of praying (18:1), as he records more instances of prayer than the other three Gospels.

The word *gospel* (meaning "good news") refers to the birth of the true king, one who came first to be a humble servant and a savior, and who will rule as the rightful king of all forever.

OUTLINE
- Jesus' birth and childhood (1–2)
- John the Baptist prepares the way (3–4)
- Jesus in Galilee (5–9)
- Jesus on the way to Jerusalem (10–18)
- Jesus in Jerusalem (19–24)

KEY VERSE
"I bring you good news that will cause great joy for all the people. Today in the town of David a Savior has been born to you; he is the Messiah, the Lord."—Luke 2:10–11

JOHN

JESUS, THE SON OF GOD

WRITTEN c. AD 85–95 by John, one of Jesus' twelve disciples and the author of 1, 2, and 3 John and Revelation, to both a Jewish and Gentile audience

PURPOSE To show Jesus as the Son of God, the Word made flesh, who provides eternal life for all who believe in him.

SUMMARY John tells us: "These are written that you may believe that Jesus is the Messiah, the Son of God, and that by believing you may have life in his name" (20:31). John's Gospel teaches us who Jesus is, and that by putting our faith in him we have eternal life.

The expression *Son of God* referred back to King David. Initially, calling Jesus "the Son of God" meant that he was Israel's king, descendant of David, the Messiah. But Jesus is not king of Israel alone. He is the King of kings and God himself in the flesh.

OUTLINE

- The Word of God (the Son) becomes flesh (1)
- First year of Jesus' ministry (first Passover) (2–4)
- Second year of Jesus' ministry (second Passover) (5)
- Third year of Jesus' ministry (third Passover) (6–11)
- Last Passover (12–19)
- Resurrection and appearances of Jesus (20–21)

KEY VERSE

"For God so loved the world that he gave his one and only Son, that whoever believes in him shall not perish but have eternal life." —John 3:16

THE BOOK OF ACTS

The book of Acts is a natural continuation of the Gospels. The good news of Jesus continues in the work of Jesus' disciples, first in Jerusalem and then throughout the world. Similar to the Historical Books in the Old Testament, Acts gives identity to God's people today by showing us how God's mission spread to all people and nations.

The Spread of Christianity in the First Century AD

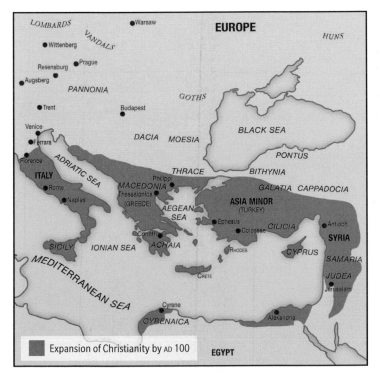

Expansion of Christianity by AD 100

ACTS
THE STORY OF THE EARLY CHURCH

WRITTEN c. AD 60–62 by Luke (also the author of the Gospel of Luke), likely a doctor and Gentile fellow traveler with Paul, to a Gentile audience

PURPOSE To record how the Holy Spirit acted through believers to spread the word of God.

SUMMARY The book of Acts picks up where the Gospel of Luke left off, with Jesus' resurrection and then ascension into heaven. Acts tells the story of what the disciples did as a response to Jesus' commissioning them to be his witnesses (Acts 1:4–5, 8). The events in Acts show how the work of the Holy Spirit in the lives of believers (the church) spreads the good news of salvation in Jesus.

Pentecost

Pentecost was a feast commemorating the giving of the Law, which gave God's people guidance, identity, strength, instruction, comfort, and light. On that feast day the disciples received the Holy Spirit, who would teach, guide, comfort, strengthen, and give light to God's people, the church.

OUTLINE
- Mission in Jerusalem (1–7)
- Mission in Judea and Samaria (8–12)
- Mission beyond Israel (13–28)

KEY VERSE
"But you will receive power when the Holy Spirit comes on you; and you will be my witnesses in Jerusalem, and in all Judea and Samaria, and to the ends of the earth." —Acts 1:8

EPISTLES

The epistles (or letters) make up twenty-one of the twenty-seven books in the New Testament. The epistles explain the effects of Jesus' ministry, the coming of the Holy Spirit, and the spread of the gospel.

The epistles are traditionally grouped into two sections:

- Paul's Epistles are the thirteen letters written by the apostle Paul (Romans through Philemon).
- The General Epistles are the eight letters written by other apostles or early church leaders (Hebrews through Jude).

EPISTLE	AUTHOR	DATE	AUDIENCE
James	James	49	Christian Jews in and around Jerusalem
Galatians	Paul	48–49	Churches in the Roman province of Galatia
1 Thessalonians	Paul	50–52	Church in the city of Thessalonica
2 Thessalonians	Paul	50–52	Church in the city of Thessalonica
1 Corinthians	Paul	55–56	Church in the port city of Corinth
2 Corinthians	Paul	56	Church in the port city of Corinth
Romans	Paul	57	Church in Rome
Philippians	Paul	60–62	Church in the important Roman colonial city of Philippi

EPISTLE	AUTHOR	DATE	AUDIENCE
Colossians	Paul	60–62	Church in Colossae (in modern-day Turkey)
Philemon	Paul	60–62	Philemon, a leader at the church in Colossae
Ephesians	Paul	60–62	Church in the Hellenistic cultural center of Ephesus
1 Timothy	Paul	62–66	Timothy, one of Paul's disciples, who was ministering in Ephesus
Titus	Paul	64–66	Titus, one of Paul's disciples, who was ministering on the island of Crete
1 Peter	Peter	64–65	Churches in Roman provinces of Asia Minor (modern-day Turkey)
2 Peter	Peter	64–65	Churches in Roman provinces of Asia Minor (modern-day Turkey)
2 Timothy	Paul	66–67	Timothy, one of Paul's disciples, who was ministering in Ephesus
Jude	Jude	60s–80s	Unknown. Perhaps addressed to Jewish Christians.
Hebrews	Unknown	60–69	Jewish Christians
1 John	John	85–95	Churches in Asia Minor
2 John	John	85–95	Probably to a house church in Asia Minor
3 John	John	85–95	Gaius, a Christian in a church in Asia Minor

Paul's Key Teachings

The apostle Paul's thirteen epistles contain essential discussions of a wide variety of topics. Here are a few of his key teachings.

SIN is the universal human condition.	*"All have sinned and fall short of the glory of God."* Romans 3:23; also Romans 1:18–32
THE LAW shows us our sin.	*"Through the law we become conscious of our sin."* Romans 3:20; also Romans 3:28; Galatians 3:1–14, 21–22
JUSTIFICATION comes through faith in Christ.	*"A person is not justified by the works of the law, but by faith in Jesus Christ."* Galatians 2:16; also Romans 5:1
THE GRACE of God saves us.	*"By grace you have been saved."* Ephesians 2:8; also Romans 5:20
RIGHTEOUSNESS is given by God.	*"This righteousness is given through faith in Jesus Christ to all who believe."* Romans 3:22; also Galatians 5:5–6; Philippians 3:9
CHRIST is Lord over all.	*"There is but one Lord, Jesus Christ."* 1 Corinthians 8:6; also Colossians 1:15–20
THE HOLY SPIRIT is believers' guide.	*"Since we live by the Spirit, let us keep in step with the Spirit."* Galatians 5:25; also Romans 8:1–17; 2 Corinthians 5:5
THE CHURCH is diverse, but unified.	*"You are the body of Christ, and each one of you is a part of it."* 1 Corinthians 12:27; also Galatians 3:28
PRAYER is essential for all believers.	*"By prayer and petition, with thanksgiving, present your requests to God."* Philippians 4:6; also Colossians 4:2; 1 Thessalonians 5:17
LOVE is the most important quality.	*"These three remain: faith, hope and love. But the greatest of these is love."* 1 Corinthians 13:13; also Colossians 3:14

ROMANS

A LETTER ABOUT THE POWER OF THE GOSPEL

WRITTEN c. AD 57 by the apostle Paul to Christians in Rome

PURPOSE To teach about law, faith, salvation, and righteous living.

SUMMARY The epistle to the Romans is Paul's most theologically complex letter. It details crucial topics of the Christian faith. But it is also a personal letter. Paul sends greetings and encourages believers in Rome to be unified and live wisely.

OUTLINE
- The power of the gospel (1–8)
- Israel and the gospel (9–11)
- The gospel in believers' lives (12–16)

Paul's encounter with Christ in Acts 9 put him on a radically new path. He went from fiercely persecuting Christians to becoming the greatest Christian missionary of all time. He authored more books of the Bible than anyone else. Paul's faith eventually cost him his life. According to tradition, Paul (along with the apostle Peter) was martyred in Rome under Emperor Nero's persecution of Christians in AD 64–68.

JESUS IN ROMANS

The letter includes Paul's presentation of the gospel. Jesus is the central figure and the climax of the gospel story. In his letter, Paul presents the power of God through Jesus: his full grace displayed in his sacrifice, and his justice fulfilled in his death and resurrection.

KEY VERSE

"Do not conform to the pattern of this world, but be transformed by the renewing of your mind." —Romans 12:2

1 CORINTHIANS

A LETTER TO CLEAR UP MISUNDERSTANDINGS

WRITTEN c. AD 55 56 by the apostle Paul to Christians in Corinth

PURPOSE To address divisions and immorality in the church, and to encourage believers to love one another.

SUMMARY There was a lot of confusion in the church at Corinth (5:9–10). Paul wrote this letter to answer questions about the issues they faced, including Christian conscience, sexual conduct, spiritual gifts, love, and the resurrection.

OUTLINE
- Divisions (1–4)
- Morality (5–11)
- Doctrine (12–15)
- Final greetings (16)

JESUS IN 1 CORINTHIANS Jesus' resurrection is at the heart of the Christian proclamation of the good news and of our faith. His resurrection gives us hope in uncertain times, courage for the times of trials, and guidance when we feel disoriented.

KEY VERSE
"Love is patient, love is kind. It does not envy, it does not boast, it is not proud."—1 Corinthians 13:4

Eyewitnesses to Jesus' Resurrection

Paul lists eyewitnesses to Jesus' resurrection in 1 Corinthians 15. Along with information from the Gospels and Acts, there were at least eleven separate appearances to over 500 individuals.

REFERENCE	EYEWITNESS
John 20:1–18	Mary Magdalene
Matthew 28:8–10; Mark 16:1; Luke 24:10	The women (probably Mary Magdalene, Mary the mother of James and Salome, Joanna, and others)
1 Corinthians 15:5	Peter
Luke 24:36–49; John 20:19–25	The Twelve minus Thomas
1 Corinthians 15:5 (probably the same as John 20:26–29)	The Twelve
Luke 24:13–35	Two on the road to Emmaus
John 21:1–25	Seven fishing on the Sea of Galilee
1 Corinthians 15:6	Five hundred believers
1 Corinthians 15:7	James the brother of the Lord
1 Corinthians 15:7 (see also Mark 16:19–20; Luke 24:50–53; Acts 1:9–11, 21–22)	All the apostles
1 Corinthians 15:8 (see also Acts 9:1–19; 22:1–18; 26:12–18)	Paul on the road to Damascus

2 CORINTHIANS
PAUL'S MOST PERSONAL LETTER

WRITTEN c. AD 56 by the apostle Paul to Christians in Corinth

PURPOSE To defend Paul's call as an apostle and to address deceivers.

SUMMARY In this letter, Paul reinforces what he wrote in 1 Corinthians and then offers a passionate defense of his ministry in the face of many attacks.

OUTLINE
- Apostleship (1–7)
- Sacrificial giving (8–9)
- False apostles (10–12)
- Final greetings (13)

JESUS IN 2 CORINTHIANS
The apostle Paul's ministry was modeled after Jesus' own ministry of reconciliation. In Paul's weakness, Christ's glory is more fully displayed. Jesus shone in Paul's suffering, was revealed in Paul's preaching, and was glorified in Paul's ministry.

Who Was Paul?

Paul was an archenemy of Christianity, who amazingly became the greatest Christian missionary of all time. He authored more books of the Bible than anyone else and is called the "apostle to the Gentiles."

KEY VERSE
"My grace is sufficient for you, for my power is made perfect in weakness." —2 Corinthians 12:9

GALATIANS

A LETTER ABOUT JUSTIFICATION BY FAITH

WRITTEN c. AD 48–49 by the apostle Paul to Christians in Galatia

PURPOSE To warn against legalism and defend justification by faith.

SUMMARY Paul defends his authority as an apostle and argues that the true gospel teaches that justification is by faith, contrary to what some false preachers in the church were saying. He urges believers to use their freedom in Christ to walk in the Spirit and not in the sinful desires of the flesh.

OUTLINE
- Paul's defense (1–2)
- Justification by faith (3–4)
- Living by the Spirit (5–6)

JESUS IN GALATIANS By the grace of God, Jesus died so that all who believe in him are saved. To suggest one is justified by anything other than faith in Jesus is corrupting the grace of God that is Jesus Christ, his death, and his resurrection.

KEY VERSE
"The fruit of the Spirit is love, joy, peace, forbearance, kindness, goodness, faithfulness, gentleness and self-control."
—Galatians 5:22–23

EPHESIANS

A LETTER ABOUT LIVING IN GOD-HONORING WAYS

WRITTEN   c. AD 60–62 by the apostle Paul to Christians in Ephesus

PURPOSE   To show believers what it means to be a follower of Christ and encourage them in their spiritual walk.

SUMMARY   Writing from a prison in Rome, Paul encourages believers in Ephesus as they face tremendous pressure to participate in the sinfulness of their surroundings. Ephesus—a cosmopolitan city with Jews, Greeks, and Romans—was known for its many pagan cults.

OUTLINE
- Grace (1)
- Reconciliation (2–3)
- Christian living (4–6)

JESUS IN EPHESIANS   Paul describes the church as the body of Christ. Our identity as believers comes by our being in and with Christ. Jesus is at the center of the identity, activity, and future of the church. God has equipped all believers to serve Christ in the world.

KEY VERSE
"For it is by grace you have been saved, through faith—and this is not from yourselves, it is the gift of God." —Ephesians 2:8

God's Riches to Believers

In his many letters, Paul often uses the phrase, "in Christ."
The letter of Ephesians contains the most examples. The
phrases "with Christ" and "through Christ" are also used.
In Christ, believers:

- Have every spiritual blessing reserved in heaven (1:3).
- Are chosen before the creation of the world to be holy and blameless (1:4, 11).
- Are predestined to be adopted as children of God (1:5, 11).
- Are given grace, have redemption and forgiveness, and receive wisdom (1:6–8).
- Are marked with God's seal of the promised Holy Spirit as a guarantee (1:13–14).
- Have resurrection power (1:19–20).
- Are made alive (2:5).
- Are created anew (2:10, 15–16).
- Are brought near to God (2:13).
- Have access to the Father through the Spirit (2:18).
- Are built and joined together into a spiritual temple (2:21–22).
- May approach God with freedom and confidence (3:12).

PHILIPPIANS
A LETTER ABOUT LIVING LIKE CHRIST

WRITTEN c. AD 60–62 by the apostle Paul to Christians in Philippi

PURPOSE To express Paul's love and affection for believers.

SUMMARY Under house arrest in Rome, Paul urges believers to "have the same mindset as Christ Jesus" (2:5) and learn to live humbly, so that there is unity in the church.

OUTLINE
- Paul's imprisonment (1)
- Living humbly like Christ (2)
- Encouragement to press on (3)
- Plea for unity (4)

JESUS IN PHILIPPIANS The view that Paul offers of Jesus in this letter is breathtaking. The glorious Lord humbled himself to become like one of us. Such humility is best demonstrated in his obedience, which led him to a gruesome death. Yet, God lifted him up (exalted him) from his humiliation and put him above all things.

KEY VERSE
". . . being confident of this, that he who began a good work in you will carry it on to completion until the day of Christ Jesus."
—Philippians 1:6

COLOSSIANS

A LETTER ABOUT THE SUPREMACY OF CHRIST

WRITTEN c. AD 60–62 by the apostle Paul to Christians in Colossae

PURPOSE To counteract false teachings about Christ and to encourage believers.

SUMMARY The church in Colossae was dealing with false teachings, including the legalism of requiring Gentile Christians to follow Jewish religious laws. Paul dispels the false teachings by emphasizing the supremacy of Christ over all human actions and philosophies.

OUTLINE
- Supremacy of Christ (1)
- Freedom in Christ (2)
- Christian living (3–4)

JESUS IN COLOSSIANS The epistle to the Colossians emphasizes Jesus' divinity in a wonderful way: "The Son is the image of the invisible God" (1:15). Since Jesus is God, he is at the center of the whole universe, and through him, God is reconciling "all things, whether things on earth or things in heaven, by making peace through his blood, shed on the cross" (1:20).

KEY VERSE
"For in Christ all the fullness of the Deity lives in bodily form. . . .
He is the head over every power and authority."
—Colossians 2:9–10

1 THESSALONIANS

A LETTER ABOUT HOPE IN THE FACE OF PERSECUTION

WRITTEN   c. AD 50–52 by the apostle Paul to Christians in Thessalonica

PURPOSE   To express Paul's care for believers and to encourage them.

SUMMARY   Paul and Silas, facing violent persecution in Thessalonica, were forced to flee the city (Acts 17:1–10). It is no wonder then that Paul spends the first three chapters of this letter discussing his actions and absence. Paul then encourages believers to live holy lives, despite enduring persecution, because Christ is coming again.

OUTLINE
- Paul's actions and absence (1–3)
- Believers who have died (4)
- The day of the Lord (5)

KEY VERSE   *"For the Lord himself will come down from heaven . . . with the trumpet call of God, and the dead in Christ will rise first."* —1 Thessalonians 4:16

Jesus in 1 & 2 Thessalonians

Jesus told his disciples that he would come again. Someday, there will be a new heaven and a new earth. When Jesus returns, we will be in God's presence forever and God will "wipe every tear from [our] eyes" (Revelation 21:4).

When Christ returns, he will put an end to all the suffering and persecution we live through now. Jesus promises us that the Holy Spirit

2 THESSALONIANS

A LETTER ABOUT BEING READY

WRITTEN   c. AD 50–52 by the apostle Paul to Christians in Thessalonica

PURPOSE   To stress the importance of being ready for Christ's return.

SUMMARY   Written about six months after Paul's first letter to the Thessalonians, this second letter echoes many themes in the first. Paul also warns believers not to be idle because everyone must be prepared for Christ's return.

OUTLINE
- Thanksgiving and prayer (1)
- Standing firm (2)
- Warnings against laziness (3)

KEY VERSE
"Stand firm and hold fast to the teachings we passed on to you."
—2 Thessalonians 2:15

will comfort and strengthen us through these difficult times (John 14). Paul writes in 2 Thessalonians, "But the Lord is faithful, and he will strengthen you and protect you from the evil one" (3:3). Jesus kept, and continues to keep, his promises to strengthen and comfort us until the day of his second coming.

1 TIMOTHY

INSTRUCTIONS FOR LEADING A CHURCH

WRITTEN c. AD 62–66 by the apostle Paul to Timothy, a young pastor in Ephesus

PURPOSE To remove false doctrine and suggest proper church leadership.

SUMMARY In this letter, Paul gives instructions to Timothy, a young pastor dealing with false teachings within the church in Ephesus.

OUTLINE
- Proper worship (1–3)
- Correct doctrine (4)
- Dealing with church members (5)
- Final instructions (6)

JESUS IN 1 TIMOTHY The letter to Timothy is a practical letter about the church, especially its life and teachings. Jesus is our Savior, our Mediator, and the Lord of the church. All worship and organization within the body falls under Jesus' Lordship.

KEY VERSE
"Don't let anyone look down on you because you are young, but set an example for the believers in speech, in conduct, in love, in faith and in purity." —1 Timothy 4:12

Timothy, whose father was a Greek and mother a Jewish Christian, traveled with Paul on his second missionary journey (Acts 16:1–5). Paul spoke very highly of Timothy, saying, "I have no one else like him, who will show genuine concern for your welfare" (Philippians 2:20).

2 TIMOTHY

A LETTER ABOUT PERSEVERING

WRITTEN c. AD 66–67 by the apostle Paul to Timothy, a young pastor in Ephesus

PURPOSE To encourage Timothy to remain faithful in ministry even in the midst of suffering.

SUMMARY Written from prison in Rome, this second letter to Timothy is perhaps Paul's last letter. Paul encourages the young pastor to persevere in preaching the gospel through hardships, and to hold fast to Scripture and guard the gospel against false teachings.

OUTLINE
- The gospel (1)
- False teachers (2)
- Preaching the word of God (3)
- Final instructions (4)

JESUS IN 2 TIMOTHY Eternal glory is the reward for all who have faith in Christ, who died and rose from the dead. Jesus is the righteous judge of everyone (2 Timothy 4:1, 8). Those who endure suffering for the sake of the gospel will someday be rewarded; those who live immoral lives and cause suffering to believers will be punished.

KEY VERSE
"All Scripture is God-breathed and is useful for teaching, rebuking, correcting and training in righteousness." —2 Timothy 3:16

TITUS

INSTRUCTIONS FOR CHURCH LEADERSHIP AND UPRIGHT LIVING

WRITTEN c. AD 64–66 by the apostle Paul to Titus, a pastor in Crete

PURPOSE To encourage Christians to do good works.

SUMMARY Titus was a Gentile convert who traveled with Paul to Jerusalem (Galatians 2:1–5). Paul left Titus in charge of the churches on the island of Crete. This letter provides instructions about responsible church leadership, correct doctrine, and godly living.

OUTLINE
- Appointing elders (1)
- Doing good works (2–3)

JESUS IN TITUS In his advice to Titus, Paul reminds us that Jesus is at the center of the gospel. Jesus is our Savior, blessed hope, and Lord. We no longer subscribe to the ways of the world. When we profess our faith in Jesus, our lives should line up according to that belief.

KEY VERSE
"God our Savior . . . saved us, not because of righteous things we had done, but because of his mercy." —Titus 3:4–5

PHILEMON

AN APPEAL FOR RECONCILIATION

WRITTEN c. AD 60–62 by the apostle Paul to Philemon in Colossae

PURPOSE To ask Philemon to forgive and accept Onesimus.

SUMMARY Philemon, a leader in the church in Colossae, was the owner of a runaway slave named Onesimus. Later, after meeting Paul and becoming a Christian, Onesimus wanted reconciliation with his old master. This letter is a direct appeal from Paul to Philemon to accept Onesimus back "no longer as a slave, but . . . as a dear brother" (verse 16).

OUTLINE (verses)
- Paul commends Philemon (1–7)
- Paul's appeal to Philemon (8–22)
- Final greetings (23–25)

JESUS IN PHILEMON Jesus said, "I have come that they may have life, and have it to the full" (John 10:10). Jesus died to provide life and freedom to all people, so that there is neither "slave or free, but Christ is all, and is in all" (Colossians 3:11).

KEY VERSE
"Perhaps the reason he was separated from you for a little while was that you might have him back forever—no longer as a slave, but better than a slave, as a dear brother." —Philemon 15–16

HEBREWS

A SUPERIOR COVENANT

WRITTEN   c. AD 60–69 by an unknown author to a Jewish Christian audience

PURPOSE   To emphasize the superiority of Christ over the old covenant.

SUMMARY   Jesus Christ is superior to the angels, the Old Testament prophets, Moses, the priesthood, and the sacrificial system. This is the message of Hebrews. Jesus' death on the cross fulfilled the Old Testament. Jesus leads his followers into God's rest, and this is a journey of faith (see chapter 11).

OUTLINE
- Supremacy of Christ (1–4)
- New covenant (5–10)
- The life of faith (11–13)

JESUS IN HEBREWS   Jesus is the supreme and superior mediator, the sinless High Priest. There is no longer a need for repeated sacrifices because Jesus is the one and only sacrifice. Jesus' sacrifice provides all who believe in him access to the holy God.

KEY VERSE
"Let us run with perseverance the race marked out for us, fixing our eyes on Jesus, the pioneer and perfecter of faith."
—Hebrews 12:1–2

Heroes of the Faith in Hebrews 11

"Now faith is confidence in what we hope for and assurance about what we do not see. This is what the ancients were commended for."
—Hebrews 11:1–2

NAME	BY FAITH...	HEBREWS REFERENCE
ABEL	He offered an acceptable sacrifice.	11:4
ENOCH	He pleased God and was taken to him.	11:5
NOAH	He built the ark.	11:7
ABRAHAM	He followed God and believed his promises.	11:8–19
SARAH	She was enabled to bear children.	11:11
ISAAC	He blessed his sons' futures.	11:20
JACOB	He blessed Joseph's sons.	11:21
JOSEPH	He spoke prophetically of the exodus.	11:22
MOSES	He kept the first Passover.	11:23–28
RAHAB	She kept the Israelite spies safe.	11:31
GIDEON	He won a great battle.	11:32–40
BARAK	He won a great battle.	11:32–40
SAMSON	He fought the Philistines.	11:32–40
JEPHTHAH	He won a great battle.	11:32–40
DAVID	He was a man after God's own heart.	11:32–40
SAMUEL	He was a prophet and judge of Israel.	11:32–40

JAMES

A LETTER ABOUT HAVING A LIVING FAITH

WRITTEN c. AD 49 by James to a Jewish Christian audience

PURPOSE To encourage believers to have faith that is active.

SUMMARY James addresses Christians who had become arrogant: showing favoritism to the wealthy, using their words to harm others, and failing to serve people in need. While salvation is by faith in Jesus, James reminds readers that having faith doesn't excuse anyone from living out that faith by doing the good things God has called them to do.

James was the half-brother of Jesus (mentioned in Galatians 1:19) who was martyred in Jerusalem for his faith in AD 62.

OUTLINE
- Perseverance (1)
- Favoritism (2:1–13)
- Faith and deeds (2:14–26)
- Words and wisdom (3)
- Humility (4)
- Patience and prayer (5)

JESUS IN JAMES Although the letter of James mentions Jesus only twice (1:1; 2:1), Jesus' wonderful Sermon on the Mount in the Gospel of Matthew shines throughout the letter.

KEY VERSE
"As the body without the spirit is dead, so faith without deeds is dead."—James 2:26

James' Use of the Sermon on the Mount

JAMES	TEACHING	MATTHEW
1:2	Joy in the midst of trials	5:10–12
1:4	Exhortation to be perfect	5:48
1:5	Asking God for good things	7:7–11
1:17	God the giver of all good things	7:11
1:20	Warnings against anger	5:22
1:22	Becoming hearers and doers of the word	7:24–27
2:5	The poor inherit the kingdom	5:3, 5
2:10	Keeping the whole law	5:19
2:13	Being merciful to receive mercy	5:7
3:12	Being known by our fruits	7:16–20
3:18	The blessings of peacemakers	5:9
4:2–3	Ask and you will receive	7:7–8
4:4	Serving God vs. friendship with the world	6:24
4:9–10	Comfort for mourners	5:4
4:11–12	Warnings against judging others	7:1–5
4:13–14	Living for today	6:34
5:2–5	Moth and rust spoiling earthly treasures	6:19

1 PETER

A LETTER ABOUT SUFFERING

WRITTEN c. AD 64–65 by the apostle Peter to Christians in Asia Minor (modern-day Turkey)

PURPOSE To call Christians to holy living even in the face of suffering.

SUMMARY As persecution of Christians increased in the time of the apostles, this letter encourages faithfulness and Christ-like behavior through very difficult circumstances.

Peter, one of Jesus' twelve disciples, was a fisherman who became a top leader in the early church. It is believed that he was crucified for his faith during Emperor Nero's persecution of Christians in Rome around AD 64–68.

OUTLINE
- Blessings (1)
- Relationships (2)
- Suffering (3)
- Holiness (4)
- Standing firm (5)

KEY VERSE
"But just as he who called you is holy, so be holy in all you do."
—1 Peter 1:15

2 PETER

A LETTER ABOUT TRUSTING THE PROPHECIES AND PROMISES OF GOD

WRITTEN c. AD 64–65 by the apostle Peter to Christians (possibly in Asia Minor)

PURPOSE To urge believers not to waver in their faith.

SUMMARY This second letter warns believers against false teachers, encourages them to grow strong in their faith, and instructs them regarding the promised return of Jesus. Peter emphasizes that the prophetic word and apostolic testimony are not human creations, but are reliable testimonies.

OUTLINE
- Our calling (1)
- False teachers (2)
- Day of the Lord (3)

KEY VERSE
"For prophecy never had its origin in the human will, but prophets, though human, spoke from God as they were carried along by the Holy Spirit." —2 Peter 1:21

Jesus in 1 & 2 Peter

Jesus gave his life for us; he knows suffering. God is with us, even in times when we feel alone and defeated. Knowing that Jesus will return gives us hope to continue being faithful and obedient to God. When Jesus returns, all our pain and suffering will be redeemed and we will be with him forever.

1 JOHN

A LETTER ABOUT LOVE

WRITTEN c. AD 85–95 by the apostle John to Christians in Asia Minor

PURPOSE To emphasize Jesus' humanity and love.

SUMMARY The longest of John's three epistles, this letter focuses on love: God's love through Jesus and our love for one another. It also refutes false teachers who were claiming Jesus only appeared to be human. Jesus was in fact fully human—and fully God.

OUTLINE
- Light, love, and truth (1–3)
- Christ in the flesh (4)
- Keeping God's commands (5)

KEY VERSE
"This is how we know what love is: Jesus Christ laid down his life for us. And we ought to lay down our lives for our brothers and sisters."—1 John 3:16

John, the Apostle

John, the younger brother of the apostle James, was called the "disciple whom Jesus loved" (John 13:23). He wrote three epistles, the Gospel of John, and Revelation. Stories suggest that he died of natural causes in Ephesus around AD 100.

2 JOHN

A LETTER ABOUT DISCERNMENT

WRITTEN c. AD 85–95 by the apostle John to "the lady chosen by God" (1:1), possibly an expression meaning "the church"

PURPOSE To warn believers against falling into deception.

SUMMARY False teachers were corrupting the gospel by denying that Jesus came in the flesh. This short letter reminds believers that love, which means walking in God's commands, also includes being discerning so Christians will not deceived by false teachings.

OUTLINE (verses)
- Love (1–6)
- False teachings (7–11)
- Final greetings (12–13)

KEY VERSE
"And this is love: that we walk in obedience to his commands."
—2 John 6

3 JOHN

A LETTER ABOUT LOVING OTHERS VS. LOVING TO BE FIRST

WRITTEN c. AD 85–95 by the apostle John to Gaius, a Christian in Asia Minor

PURPOSE To praise Gaius for his loyalty and criticize Diotrephes for his pride.

SUMMARY This third letter—the shortest book in the New Testament—was written to commend Gaius for his love, faithfulness, and hospitality, but also to denounce Diotrephes for acting arrogantly, gossiping, and refusing to welcome other believers.

OUTLINE (verses)
- John commends Gaius (1–8)
- John rebukes Diotrephes (9–10)
- Final greetings (11–14)

KEY VERSE
"I have no greater joy than to hear that my children are walking in the truth." —3 John 4

Jesus in 1, 2 & 3 John

Jesus came to this world in the flesh and he died for the forgiveness of sins and the salvation of those who believe in him. When we believe in Jesus we are adopted into God's family. We are God's beloved children. As God's children, we love and obey God our Father and we love our fellow brothers and sisters and treat them with kindness and hospitality.

JUDE

A LETTER ABOUT CONTENDING FOR THE FAITH

WRITTEN AD 60s–80s (date unknown) by Jude to Christians everywhere

PURPOSE To warn against false teachers.

SUMMARY Jude—Jesus' half-brother, mentioned in Matthew 13:55 (aka "Judas")—penned this short letter to encourage believers to "contend for the faith" (verse 3). False teachers had come into the church seeking to "pervert the grace of our God into a license for immorality" (verse 4).

OUTLINE (verses)
- Greetings (1–4)
- False teachers (5–19)
- Final greetings (20–25)

JESUS IN JUDE Jesus protects us and helps us reach the goal to be in his presence. While our task is to remain aware and cautious of false teachings, Christ gives us the strength to be faithful.

KEY VERSE
"To him who is able to keep you from stumbling and to present you before his glorious presence without fault and with great joy."
—Jude 24

THE BOOK OF REVELATION

The book of Revelation is a type of writing known as *apocalyptic literature*. Apocalyptic literature reveals God's plans that were hidden to humanity. The message is conveyed through signs, symbols, dreams, and visions.

Despite many disagreements about the meaning of the book, there are important agreements among Christians:

- The message of the book is relevant for Christians today.
- The book's purpose is to provide *hope* and *encouragement* for believers.
- The book is clear on three points:

    1. Christ is coming back and will judge humanity.

    2. The powers of evil are doomed before Christ.

    3. God promises a wonderful future for all who believe in Christ.

REVELATION

VISIONS THAT REVEAL GOD'S GLORY AND TRIUMPH

WRITTEN c. AD 85–95 by the apostle John on the island of Patmos to seven churches in Asia Minor (modern-day Turkey)

PURPOSE To give hope to persecuted Christians and to provide a vision of Christ's return.

SUMMARY Christians in John's day faced severe persecution. The messages in Revelation remind believers that even when evil seems so strong, God is in control of history. God will ultimately defeat Satan and his forces. The Lord will renew his creation and live among his people.

OUTLINE
- Vision of Christ (1)
- Seven churches, seals, trumpets, histories, and bowls (2–16)
- Fall of Babylon (17–18)
- Visions of the end (19–21)
- Invitation to come (22)

JESUS IN REVELATION In his visions of heaven, John sees Jesus as he is: the ascended and glorified Lord, who is worthy of all worship. His promises to give rest and peace to his followers will be fulfilled in the new heavens and the new earth.

KEY VERSE
"He who testifies to these things says, 'Yes, I am coming soon.' Amen. Come, Lord Jesus." —Revelation 22:20

MADE EASY

by Rose Publishing

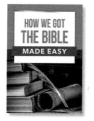

HOW WE GOT THE BIBLE MADE EASY
Key events in the history of the Bible

UNDERSTANDING THE HOLY SPIRIT MADE EASY
Who the Holy Spirit is and what he does

BIBLE TRANSLATIONS MADE EASY
Compares 20 popular Bible versions

KNOWING GOD'S WILL MADE EASY
Answers to tough questions about God's will

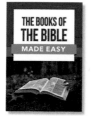

THE BOOKS OF THE BIBLE MADE EASY
Quick summaries of all 66 books of the Bible

BIBLE STUDY MADE EASY
A step-by-step guide to studying God's Word

WORLD RELIGIONS MADE EASY
30 religions and how they compare to Christianity

SHARING YOUR FAITH MADE EASY
How to share the gospel

www.hendricksonrose.com